GETTING *lucky* NUMBER SEVEN

A Taking Shots Novel

CINDI MADSEN

Entangled Publishing, LLC
2614 South Timberline Road
Suite 109
Fort Collins, CO 80525
Visit our website at www.entangledpublishing.com.

Embrace is an imprint of Entangled Publishing, LLC.

Edited by Alycia Tornetta
Cover design by Sommer Stein with Perfect Pear Creative
Covers
Cover art by iStock

Manufactured in the United States of America

First Edition April 2015

embrace

To Amanda, who encourages me to be brave and is there when I have panic attacks over it. And for just always being there.

Chapter One

LYLA

Ever notice that drunk people are, like, the worst whisperers ever? The guys were in the kitchen, getting more drinks and discussing my roommate's nice ass in what I'm sure they thought were hushed tones, while she and her friend, Kristen, were in the hallway behind me, whispering about condoms.

And I was sitting in the middle of the couch, feeling like I totally didn't belong, as usual.

I wished Einstein wasn't a scaredy-cat who'd taken off for my bedroom at the knock on the door. At least then I could pull him onto my lap and keep my hands busy petting him, although I was pretty sure focusing on my adorable gray and white puffball wasn't the kind of thing I should do while on a first date.

When Whitney and Kristen had first burst into the

apartment and told me we were going to have a group date tonight, I'd begged off. My research paper comparing generic and brand name drugs wasn't going to write itself. But then Whitney had made a compelling argument.

"Come on, Lyla, you haven't even been out, much less on a date, since your boyfriend dumped you two months ago. It's getting pathetic."

I'd wanted to say that, one, the breakup was mutual and amicable, and two, I'd been out *lots* of times. Not to parties, or clubs, or bars, or... Okay, so the past several weeks had gotten away from me, but they'd been spent studying, either here, the coffee shop on campus — which was technically out, in my opinion — or the library. Also out. I wasn't pathetic, I had a full course load, and if I didn't get stellar grades, I'd lose my scholarship. But yeah, technically speaking, the dating side of my life was non-existent since Miles and I had broken up over Thanksgiving break, and I could see how that might be the tiniest bit pathetic.

"There are three of them, too," Kristen had added. "It'd be super weird if you weren't here. Don't worry, we'll watch a movie or something, and it'll be totally chill. Nothing to be afraid of."

Afraid — I really hated that word, mostly because it so often drove my decisions. Tried and true were highly preferable, but more and more, clinging to the familiar made me feel like I was stuck in a rut. Everyone had moved on and changed, including Miles, and I was still the same.

The three boys who showed up at our apartment were cute, although there didn't seem to be much going on between the ears or underneath the muscles. Then again, since my brain had frozen up every time I tried to say anything to

Colin, the guy I was supposed to be on a date with, I couldn't really talk. Literally. I use the term "date" loosely, too, since so far there'd only been a lot of drinking with the other two couples cuddling and flirting and me doing the struggling-for-words thing. I had nodding down to a science, though.

Kristin and Whitney erupted in giggles as they stuffed their pockets with condoms they'd retrieved from the bathroom, and then I heard Colin say, "Why'd I get stuck with the fugly, boring one?"

The smile I had plastered on my face turned to glass and cracked. I gripped the cell phone I'd just been checking my assignment to-do list on, the hard case digging into my skin.

"Be nice," one of the guys whispered at a drunken decibel level of stealthiness. "Maybe she'll let you get to second base. Who knows what she's hiding underneath all those clothes? Sometimes the quiet ones are the kinkiest."

Everything inside of me shriveled up and died, and I stared at the coffee table where my notebook and research articles still were, Colin's awful words echoing through my brain. It wasn't the first time I'd been mocked about my clothes or called something less than flattering—"nerd" and "weirdo" had been faux-whispered under breaths as I was passed by in high school halls plenty of times. For some stupid reason, I thought college would be different. Wasn't this supposed to be where I met mature guys? Where people thought smart was sexy?

I nearly jumped when Colin sat next to me and offered me a cup. "Sure you don't want one?"

A lump rose in my throat, along with tears. Whitney and Kristen were already draped across their dates, tongue-action seconds from recommencing.

"No thanks." I looked down at my phone. "Oh, I'm getting a call. Guess I didn't realize it's on silent. I really should get it." I held it up to my ear. "What? You need me to come get you? Where are—"

My ringtone suddenly blared into my ear, and I dropped my phone. It tumbled slowly, catching in the scarf around my neck for a moment before sliding down my long skirt and clattering against the floor. It continued to vibrate against the hard wood, and I scrambled to pick it up. Hardly anyone called me. I lifted it and stared at the display.

My mom.

Of course.

Heat flooded my face, and Colin was looking at me with his eyebrows scrunched. Actually, everyone was looking at me with pretty much the same expression.

"I guess the call dropped, but I didn't realize, so…" I lamely gestured at the phone. I couldn't answer and talk to my mom, and I couldn't stay here. "Anyway, I have to go. Sorry."

I grabbed my keys and rushed out the door. The icy Boston air slapped me in the face, reminding me I should've grabbed my coat, but it was too late for that now. As soon as I made it to the safety of my car, tears broke free. It was bad enough to be called fugly and boring, but I, Lyla Wilder, couldn't even make a smooth exit. No, I had to go and take awkward to the next level.

Times like these were when I really missed having a boyfriend who was also slightly awkward. Miles had made me feel normal, and when I was with him, it was easier to ignore insults and to keep from thinking about how few friends I had. I understood why it'd been time to break up—long-distance was just too hard, especially when he and I were both slaves to our studies. I thought about calling him now, just to have a friendly shoulder to cry on, but that'd only make missing him—and the way things used to be—worse.

I glanced at my apartment door on the second floor. *Who knows how long they'll be up there?* Knowing my roommate and her equally boy-crazy friend, it'd be a while. *No way can I go back inside tonight.*

Maybe not ever.

Ugh. I am *pathetic.*

More tears blurred my eyes as I fired up my car and cranked the heater to high. There was only one place I could think of going. I knew it was a long shot that he'd even be home on a Saturday night. And if he were, there was even less of a chance he was alone.

That was the downside of having a friend who also happened to be a hot, man-whore hockey player.

Chapter Two

BECK

My lips hovered over Monica's as I debated my next move. I'd ignored my ringing phone, because, well, I had my hands full with Monica. The knock on the door wasn't quite as easy to ignore, especially when accompanied by Lyla's voice.

"Beck, are you home? I'm having a bit of an emergency."

As soon as I sat back on the couch, Monica's eyes flashed. "Are you *kidding* me?"

Was I? Shit, I was as revved up as she was, but what was I supposed to do? Leave Lyla out on my doorstep? When it came to her, "a bit of an emergency" could be that she'd gotten a B, there was a cat in need of saving, or a slasher was after her. She really only spoke in one level, and that was "quiet." "Give me just a sec."

Monica gripped my shirt and ran her tongue over my jaw, which I'm sure she thought was sexy, but left me feeling like I'd been licked by a Labrador. "Don't keep me waiting."

Much-needed cool air hit me as soon as I opened the door. Lyla stood on the walkway, arms wrapped around herself. She didn't have on a coat, just a long-sleeved shirt and one of her multi-colored scarves. "Hey, I'm kinda busy," I said. "Can we—"

I froze at the sight of her splotchy tear-streaked cheeks. "What happened? Did someone hurt you?"

She shook her head and blew out a white puff of air. "Not physically, anyway."

I glanced from her to Monica, who was draped across the couch, wearing only her bra and jeans. Damn, she was gonna be pissed.

Lyla glanced inside and her eyes went wide. "You're obviously busy—I knew you would be. It's nothing, really. I'll just see you tomorrow for movie night, 'kay?" She turned to go, and I reached out and caught her arm.

"Come on inside." There was no way I could focus now. Sure, it'd only take a few minutes to get back into things with Monica, but I'd worry about Lyla off and on all night. Somewhere along the way, I'd started to feel responsible for her, and if anyone hurt her, I'd personally hunt them down.

After I closed the door behind us, bringing this Saturday night to a three-way kind of sitch—and not the good kind—I ran a hand through my hair. "Uh, Monica, we're going to have to catch up another time."

The girl looked Lyla up and down with a disgusted scowl on her face that screamed *You're choosing* her *over* me? and it suddenly got that much easier to say good-bye.

"In your dreams, asshole," she spat at me as she walked past. So no love lost there. I still walked her out, even though my thighs burned from tonight's game, and it involved too many stairs, because I like to think I'm at least half a gentleman.

When I got back inside, Lyla looked up from her spot on the couch. "How'd the flavor of the week take it?"

I flopped next to her, flinching when I bumped the side where I'd been checked earlier tonight. Dude thought he was real tough, but I ended up with the puck and the score—it made any resulting bruises worth it. "Actually, I met her *three* weekends ago, thank-you-very-much."

"Ooh, a repeat offender. I'm impressed."

"I can hear you judging me. Pretty harsh after the cock blocking. Guess I'll just have to make do with you." I leaned toward her, mouth open as wide as I could get it, tongue out.

"Ew!" She laughed and shoved me away. Good. She was smiling now. The sad face was killing me. But all too soon, it was back. If it were anyone else, I would run as far as I could go to keep from discussing emotions or getting into whatever had made her cry. But Lyla was my girl, and like I said, I felt responsible for her. Probably because hanging with her was always easy—the break from life I occasionally needed—and I didn't have many close friends who knew me as well as she did. I liked it that way, and honestly, I wasn't sure how she'd managed to get in so easily.

"Spill it."

She ran her palms down her thighs, focusing on the motion. "I got set up on a date tonight. Or more like I was the sixth wheel pity-date option."

"Sixth wheel?" I asked.

She told me about the set-up, the drinking, and when she looked down and whispered the part about some asshole calling her fugly and boring, I clenched my fists, wanting to find the guy and use them on him. "I just don't think I can go back tonight." She wiped the tears from her cheeks. "Can I crash on your couch?"

"You know you can. Anytime." Over the past few months I'd forgotten how fragile she could be. She had no problem speaking her mind around me anymore, but it'd taken a while, and sometimes I worried people would take advantage of her. I'd never expected someone to go out of his way to be outright mean, though. "That guy was wrong, Lyla. He's clearly a giant douche."

She unwound the scarf from her neck and tossed it aside. Then she pulled her light brown waves into a messy bun, took a pencil off the side table, and shoved it through her hair to secure it in place. "I don't think I'm quite as bad as fugly, but I am plain. And I am boring. All I ever do is study. Just like I did in high school. I thought I'd go to college and live in a big city, and things would be different. Only everyone else is different, and I'm as awkward and nerdy as ever. That whole things-get-better-after-high-school is total crap."

I didn't even know where to start with that. Seemed like a lot of landmines that could explode if I said the wrong thing.

"I'm sick of it, Beck. I don't want to do the safe thing anymore just because I'm too afraid to try anything else." Resolve set into her features—it was the same look she got when we were solving difficult chemistry equations last semester, or when one of our labs didn't go quite right and we needed to figure out why. She got scary-focused sometimes. "It's time for a change. Time to let loose a little. I'm in my second semester of college, and I haven't done anything you're supposed to do. Like get so drunk you puke and don't remember the rest of the night."

"Overrated, I swear."

She looked at me, that deadly look on her face, and I held up my hands. "Fine. You wanna get drunk and puke, I'm not gonna stop you."

"But I want to do, like, more than just drinking." Her brow furrowed and I could practically see the wheels in her brain spinning. "I should make a list and outline a plan."

I was going to point out that list-making wasn't the best way to let loose, but I decided to let it go.

She leaned forward and glanced around. "Don't you have any other pens or pencils?"

"I'm surprised I had the one you put in your hair. If you really need something to write with, I can grab a pen from the kitchen."

"And a piece of paper?"

As if she'd ever use just one—another thing I'd learned when we'd shared a class. So instead of the kitchen, I headed into my bedroom, grabbed a mostly blank notebook and pen, and handed them over. She tapped the pen to her lips. "I'm thinking I start with a new look—like one of those extreme makeovers. It'll get me in a new mind frame, so I can be a whole new me. What do you think? Would I look okay super blond? Or should I go dark? Or maybe streaky highlights?" Her eyebrows arched as she looked up from the blank paper.

Girls loved these kinds of trick questions, and I'd learned to tread carefully whenever they came up. "I think you look fine the way you are."

She tilted her head and sighed. "But what did you think

when you first met me? You can be honest. I'm sure you were a little disappointed when you found out I was your assigned chem partner."

"Well, yeah," I said, "but that was because with how damn cute you were, I was sure you'd be stupid, and that meant I was going to end up doing all the work." She rolled her eyes, and I smiled, unable to keep from adding, "Then I caught your scent, and your blood smelled so good, I was afraid I'd kill you and eat you. That's why I was all broody and denting the table the first day."

Lyla laughed and shoved my arm. "You're stupid."

"I am. I let you talk me into that *Twilight* marathon last Sunday. Clearly a mistake."

"Hey, I watched that dumb prank movie with the gross bathroom humor. And we still have two *Twilight* movies to go. Now, be serious."

"Okay. Serious." I draped my arm behind the couch and met her gaze. "Changing your look because of what some asshole said is stupid." I wasn't lying when I said she was damn cute—she had a sweet, innocent look about her, and I'd always liked that she was unique. "And doesn't it go against your feminist values?"

Her lips turned into a pouty frown. "It's not against feminism to look my best. And I'm not changing it for *him*. I'm changing it for me." She put a hand over her heart. "*I* want to try new things. I spent high school playing things safe. Being the perfect girl with perfect grades that my parents wanted me to be so I could get into a great college. But here I finally am, and I don't want to be the nice girl anymore. I want to be the hot girl. I want to be bolder. Do something completely crazy. Dangerous, even."

The glint in her eyes was definitely dangerous, and there were alarm bells going off in my head. "I don't want to look back and have all these regrets," she said, her voice firm and louder than usual. "And if I don't do it this semester, before my classes get even more difficult and I'm totally set in my boring patterns, it'll be that much harder." She pulled one corner of her bottom lip between her teeth, looking vulnerable again. "But I'll admit I'm completely out of my league here. In order to do this, I need your help."

I stared into her hazel eyes, so full of hope and determination, and my heart tugged. One day we'd been partners for chem lab, and then before I knew it, she was the girl who talked me into watching chick flicks and interrupted make-out sessions with no repercussions. She'd looked so harmless, too, with her hippie style and messy bun with a pen or pencil forever stabbed through it.

"Please," she added, putting her hands up in prayer position.

If it was what she really wanted, of course I was going to help her. After all, what were friends for?

Chapter Three

A sense of desperation filled me as Beck just stared, his mouth set in a firm line. Suddenly I felt suffocated by everything I hadn't done yet—I was sick of playing it safe, of being the quiet one who never tried anything and kept from rocking the boat at all costs. I didn't want to be boring, and I didn't want to be afraid. I wanted to jump into the fog, not knowing where it was going to lead me. I wanted to forget about who I was in high school, shake off my gloom over my *mutual* breakup with Miles, and have the adventurous college experience that other people my age were having.

But I wasn't delusional enough to think I could pull it off by myself—that was like the blind leading the blind. Or whatever it was when there was just one struggling clueless person without a life preserver to fall back on.

Beck sighed and said, "Okay. I'll help however I can."

A squeal escaped my lips as I hugged him. "Thanks. You're the best."

"Uh-huh." Beck liked to act tough, and I'll admit when I first met him, I was totally intimidated by the height and muscles and natural charm. My knees actually wobbled a little the first time he aimed his smile at me, despite my previous assertions that I'd never understood the attraction to cocky jocks.

Funnily enough, when I'd been assigned as his lab partner I'd also thought I was going to have to do most of the work—not that I bought for a second Beck had actually thought that. He was smarter than I expected, not to mention friendlier, and after a couple weeks of doing experiments and homework together, I was less focused on the muscles and perfectly messy golden hair, and more focused on how well we worked together. He was so clearly out of my league on every level, I was surprised at how easily we became friends.

When I had a bad day, he knew how to joke it away, and when Miles and I broke up, Beck had helped take my mind off it. Movie and ice cream Sundays had become one of our traditions, and after a long week of studying, it was the perfect way to unwind. I knew that most of his other days and nights were filled with hockey and girls, and sometimes I still marveled that he set apart an evening for us to hang out and fight over which movie to watch next.

"Okay, mister a-year-older-and-wiser, what are the things I need to experience to make this whole college experience complete?" I pulled the notebook closer to me, and wrote the one I already knew I desperately needed:

1. New edgier look

"I figure I should start slow and work up to the big stuff. What's a good drinking goal? I mean, I don't really want to wake up somewhere and not know how I got there. That's too far. But I wanna get, like, *really* drunk. See what it's like. And I want to do something at a party that's bold. More than just sipping from a red cup all night, but not embarrassing myself to the point I'll never live it down."

Beck ran a couple of fingertips along his jaw. "How about, 'Do a keg stand?' Gets you drunk and grabs attention. Two birds, one stone."

2. Do a keg stand (Remember to not wear a skirt that night.)

I pointed at the item I'd just added. "I don't want *that* much attention, and I'm pretty sure trying to hold down my skirt so I don't flash everyone while trying to drink would be too much stress. Hopefully, if I do one thing at a time, I won't have a panic attack over it."

Two creases formed between Beck's eyebrows, and I could see the doubt flickering across his features. I put my hand on his arm. "I want to do this. But I'm also me. Just help me figure out a happy medium. And a place to do a keg stand and get super drunk. Do you know of any parties in the near future?"

"Pretty sure we could find a number of options next Friday or Saturday."

"Ooh, that'll be perfect, because it gives me time to get my new edgy look in order. We'll go shopping this week."

"*We'll?*" Beck's lip curled. "Don't you know? Guys don't like shopping."

"I think we've already established that I need help figuring out what guys like. That's why you're helping me, remember?" Which led me to decide that number three should be something bold involving a guy.

3. Go to a party and flirt with a total stranger

Beck read over my shoulder and made a *hmm* noise.

"What?" I asked. "That's wussy in college, isn't it? It needs to be more than flirt. Oh, jeez, this is going to be tricky, because I'm *really* bad at that kind of thing. My brain and my mouth get disconnected when I see hot guys and then I just sorta blink or say stupid things."

"You've uh…" Beck rubbed the back of his neck. I so rarely saw him flustered that anxiety automatically tightened my stomach. He didn't think I could pull it off. Maybe he was right, and there was no amount of help that'd turn me into a girl who could snag a guy. Miles was just a fluke — I bet he wasn't even so much attracted to me as to my brain and my ambition. "If this is some quest to lose your virginity, I'm out, Ly. There's too high a risk of it going badly, and then I'll feel responsible and — "

"*No*." Heat flooded my cheeks. "I dated Miles for over two years. We…you know. This 'quest' is about having goals that have nothing to do with grades or a future career. My relationship with Miles is a perfect example of having a nice, safe relationship but not a lot of surprises, or excitement, or…passion. Not that…" I shook my head. How'd we even get here?

Beck patted my knee. "It's okay. I don't need details. I just thought I should check before fully diving into this harebrained scheme of yours."

I crossed out my original number three.

~~3. Go to a party and flirt with a total stranger~~

3. *Make out with someone I don't know (exact level of making out TBD as the kissing happens)*

"Better?" I asked.

"Better," Beck said, a crooked smile with a hint of mocking me on his lips.

"I know you think I'm being silly, but I want to know what it's like to go out and flirt and kiss a guy without having any expectations—no steady dating, no getting serious. That way I'm open to whatever adventure awaits around the corner." The more I thought about it, the surer I became that this was a brilliant plan. I set the notebook on the coffee table. "I'll come up with more items later, then you can help me modify them as needed. First things first. Get your laptop so I can go online and look up hairstyles."

"Make me some pancakes."

I smacked Beck's arm. "You can't demand I make you pancakes. *That's* against my feminist values."

Beck swiped his hand in front of him, as if he were clearing the air of the madness I dared to put out there. "Wait? You can order me around, but I"—he touched two fingers to his chest—"can't do it back?"

"Now you're getting it." I kicked off my shoes and crossed my legs on his cushy couch, spreading out my skirt so everything was covered. Now that he'd mentioned food, my stomach was starting to rumble. "Let's order pizza."

Beck made a face like I'd suggested eating roasted

worms or something. "Not tomato and green pepper. I can sorta understand the peppers, but there's already tomatoes in the sauce. Why order more?"

I sighed. "We've been over this a hundred times, and like those past hundred times, it's because it involves different textures and seasonings, and I just like it, so I shouldn't have to justify my choice. I don't ask you to explain your carnivore madness."

"Because it needs no explanation."

"Just get it on half like we always do."

He was already pulling out his phone, most likely getting ready to dial up our usual pizza place—I hoped anyway. Now that pizza had been mentioned, my stomach would be happy with nothing else. "But then you never eat all of your half," he complained. "And the next day I have to pick off the disgusting tomatoes and eat it while wishing there were some meat on there."

"Your life is tragically hard. Deal with it and bring me your laptop." I flashed him an over-the-top grin. "Please with pepperoni on top? I'll even let you add sausage to my half of the pizza."

"And she learns how to compromise," he said in a loud, announcer-type voice. "Check off that item."

"Yeah, I think that's the opposite of being bold."

"Ah, but it *is* what guys want." He grinned and nudged me with his elbow. "You're gonna be a pro at this in no time."

I certainly hoped so. Because it was also going to require using the credit card I got *in case of emergency ONLY*.

Right now my life was in a state of disaster, though, and if I weren't mistaken, that was pretty much the same as an emergency.

Chapter Four

Some people swam, some ran, some liked to get all Zen and do yoga or meditation. I preferred slamming guys into walls. I checked my defender, and when he was sliding down the glass of the hockey rink, I hit the puck and skated after it, heading toward the goal.

This was my place where everything else disappeared. Classes got boring and my mind tended to drift, and I rarely liked where it went these days. I guess if you put off dealing with things long enough, they simply came after you when you least wanted them to.

I swung my hockey stick back, aimed to the left of the goalie, and hit for everything I was worth. Charlie tried to catch it, but he missed, and it soared in.

I threw my hands up as my teammates barreled into me. Then Coach called practice and we headed toward the locker room. Just as I was about to leave, I remembered Lyla and her damn goals. I got where she was coming from, and I thought loosening up a bit might be good for her, but she was also sweet and naïve enough to get herself into trouble, and I was determined to make sure the trouble didn't get out of control, even if that's what she thought she wanted.

"Hey, any of you know if there's a party going on this weekend?"

"My frat's having one," Daniel said.

A big *hell no* to that. Frat boys and Lyla screamed bad idea. Daniel wasn't a bad guy, but most of the other dudes he lived with were pricks who cared about name brand clothing, fancy cars, and girls who looked like Victoria's Secret models.

Carson slammed his locker door. "There's one at the Quad. There's guaranteed to be lots of beer and pretty girls."

"What about guys?" I asked, and Carson looked at me like I'd sprouted a unicorn horn. "Not for me, dumbass. I've got a friend, and she's looking to party."

"Send her to me, and I'll take *good* care of her."

Another *hell no*. He slept with more girls than I did. Honestly, though, that wasn't even that hard, despite what people tended to assume about me. Sex usually led to attachments, which was why I lived in a constant state of frustration, only closing the deal with girls I knew wouldn't constantly call and follow me around. Not that I hadn't misjudged before, but I tried. Carson promised girls they were special and then treated them like shit. He wasn't going near Lyla.

But the party at the Quad was probably the better pick of the two. I'd keep asking, just in case something better came up. I don't know what more I was looking for—keg stand opportunities were a dime a dozen. Hopefully we could knock out Lyla's first two items at once, and then she could get it out of her system and go back to being happy. Seemed like she'd been sadder the past few months, ever since she and her boyfriend broke up, immediately followed by dealing with finals. I'd chalked it up to stress, but maybe there was more going on.

"Text me the details," I said, then headed out of the locker room. As I walked to my Land Rover, I checked my phone. There was a text from Monica saying she wanted to meet up tonight—apparently I'd been forgiven.

Just as I was about to text back and tell her to meet me at my place, my phone rang. It was Lyla, so I answered. "Yeah?"

"I was hoping you could come pick me up so we could go to the mall. I really need to get moving on my first item."

For a moment I thought about telling her I was serious about the no shopping thing. The whole point of moving into an apartment by myself and keeping my schedule filled with weight training, hockey practices, and games was so that I didn't have to deal with people unless it was on my terms. So that no one saw when the past rose up and got the best of me. And if I went, this would be the second time I let her get between me and getting laid. Monica was a no-strings-attached girl, and they weren't exactly easy to find. I couldn't imagine choosing shopping when sex was an option.

But then I pictured Lyla's sad face, and thought of all the times she'd cheered me up when I was having a shit day. "I've got to shower and change. Give me like thirty or forty."

• • •

"What about this?" Lyla asked, moving aside the pink and purple scarf she had on and holding a black shirt over her white sweater. "Or is it too boring? I usually wear a lot of colors, but maybe that's too much? Maybe I should just go with one solid color. Or do I go black? Do guys care either way?"

I glanced at the uniform-colored tops. I'd never thought much about it, but they did seem plain next to Lyla's usual outfits—funny since "plain" was apparently the problem she was trying to fix. I'd never seen anyone wear as many layers as she did, rain or shine. She had a scarf in every combination of colors, and nearly all of her skirts and dresses were wild prints with lots of color. "So no more hippie style?"

"Hippie?" She stuck out her lower lip in a way that made me think I'd said the wrong thing. "I'd call it more bohemian chic. A little more artsy and less peace, free love, and no showering?"

I just stared at her for a moment. "Oh. Pardon me." Come to think of it, she did look more like she should be an art student than a hardcore chemistry nerd. But I supposed I looked like a dumb jock, and I preferred to let people assume that was all there was to me. Less questions that way. "I'm the wrong person for this, Ly. You need someone who knows more about fashion."

"Okay, no pressure and all, but you're kinda one of my only friends here. And I don't need someone who knows fashion—I need a *guy's* opinion. I want to know what guys prefer for girls to wear, versus what they hate. Like, turtlenecks, or whatever."

I wrinkled my nose. "Yeah, turtlenecks are a no."

"See," she said. "You know the important stuff. And

if I try on something that guys usually like, but I can't pull off, I need you to tell me that, too. You always give it to me straight."

Not turning that "give it to me straight" comment into an innuendo wasn't easy, but I let it go. She'd probably be horrified or smack me, and while she was trying to act like this was totally normal, I could tell by the slight hitch in her voice and the way her eyes never landed on anything for more than a couple seconds that she was getting overwhelmed.

"It's pretty simple, actually," I said. "Guys like seeing girls' bodies. Accentuate what you got, hide what you don't. Lesser men might be intimidated by all of your layers and colors—I personally find them charming."

"But you don't want to date me, either." She waved her hands. "Not that I want to date you. We're, like, nonentities to each other. I get that, and that's what's so great about us. I'm just saying that I'm glad you find them charming, but I want to see if I can make a guy stop and stare here and there. I want to use what I got."

I exhaled, feeling totally out of my league. The foreboding prickling sensation warned me I was getting sucked into a conversation where I'd inevitably say the wrong thing. "Well, what do you got, then?"

She took a step toward me. "I don't know. You tell me."

Honestly, I'd never looked at her like that. I mean, of course there was the general noticing that she had nice ivory skin, a cute little nose, and a really great smile. There was also something hot-librarian about when she wore her glasses and had her hair in a bun. But she wasn't a hookup type of girl, and when I'd met her, she'd talked about Miles. A *lot*. It was one reason I hadn't hesitated to have her over to study at my place.

One day she noticed *The Hangover* DVD on my entertainment center, remarked that she hadn't seen it, and I insisted we watch it. The next week she suggested a movie, and even brought over a carton of ice cream. From there, we started our Sunday night ritual. For so long, she'd been a—as she put it—"nonentity," that I hadn't thought about what kind of body she was hiding underneath her many layers of clothes since I'd first met her.

I grabbed a few short skirts and skimpy tops and thrust them at her. "Put these on and we'll see."

She glanced at what I'd grabbed, changed the sizes out, and headed to the dressing room.

My phone rang, and I pulled it out of my pocket, thinking it was Monica, and already trying to come up with an excuse for why I'd blown her off.

But it wasn't Monica. It was the only other girl on the planet I'd ever let drag me to a mall.

Chapter Five

They always say dressing rooms have the worst lighting and mirrors, and right now, I was hoping whoever "they" were, knew what they were talking about. Why wouldn't stores invest in fabulous lighting and mirrors that smoothed out flaws? Wouldn't that sell more clothes?

"Lyla?" It was Beck, obviously. I'd heard him talking on the phone a moment ago, although I couldn't make out the words. Whoever it was, she'd immediately gotten a sweet tone I'd never heard him use before.

"Just a second," I called, tugging at the hemline of the skirt. If guys wanted to see girls' bodies, well, this getup certainly accomplished that. I hadn't worn a skirt that didn't brush my ankles since a band concert in high school that required boring black and knee-length. This one was black, showed off lots of thigh, and was more adventurous than boring—the adventure being maybe I'd accidentally flash everyone. Wahoo!

The beaded purple top scooped low, showing off quite a bit of cleavage. And by quite a bit, I mean *holy hell balls*, that's a lot of boobage. I had a lot of it to show off, too, which, trust me, I wasn't one to brag about. I'd actually wished for not-so-much many times through the years, but especially when I was younger and they were the bane of my existence.

When I'd suddenly developed at eleven, way before the rest of my friends, my mom freaked out and bought me lots of super high-necked shirts and jackets. Since she made a point to always tell me—with a frown on her face, no less— if there was even a hint of cleavage or if my shirt was "so tight it's graphic," it only added to the stress. She warned me guys would think I was older, and that I'd have to be careful. Didn't want to give them the wrong idea. Didn't want to make myself a target. I heard about it so much that I got paranoid about it. Then I found scarves, and they at least made my boring, high-necked T-shirts look cuter.

"I'm sorry to do this," Beck said through the door, "but something came up. I need to go."

The girl who'd been on the phone. My heart dropped. Of course he'd choose her over helping me shop. I didn't blame him, but it still stung a little—didn't he get how important this was to me? I stripped off the revealing clothes and started to pull my long sweater and leggings back on.

"If you want to keep shopping, maybe Whitney could come get you? Or you can catch the bus?" His voice got closer, and I saw his Adidas under the stall. "I know that sucks, though, and I swear I wouldn't leave if it wasn't important."

Maybe I wasn't the only damsel currently in distress that

Beck had to attend to. For all I knew he had needy friends like me spread across campus—he rarely talked about anything but hockey, with the occasional remark about his classes, but I knew he had more than that going on.

"Maybe I'll just catch the bus, then. It's not that far of a ride to my apartment." I cracked open the door, wishing I'd left the outfit on so he could've told me if it was a go or not. He looked a little paler than usual, and the lines in his forehead were creased. "Everything okay?"

"Yeah, no worries." His attempted smile didn't fully catch hold. He glanced at the discarded skirt and shirt bunched up on the floor. "How'd they look?"

"Skimpy."

"Well, that's the opposite of nice and sweet. I say go with it. Just act confident and you can pull off anything."

"Confidence." I gave one sharp nod, even though confidence had always been a hard thing for me when it came to anything besides school. "Got it."

He took my hand and squeezed it, calming the worries rising up to tell me that I'd never be able to even fake that much confidence. "Thanks again for being so cool. I'll catch you later." His gaze remained on me as he backed away from the dressing room. "And I found us a party to go to, so start your preparations, because I know you've got some kind of checklist typed up."

"I don't." Yet. That was tonight's activity. "Is there anything I should put on there, though? If I decide to make one?"

Beck gave me an I-knew-it grin. "Don't overanalyze, and don't stress. Buy yourself that outfit, and I'll take care of everything else."

He nearly bumped into the attendant who'd come in, only he somehow sensed her right before contact, confirming my suspicion that he might be part ninja. She beamed at him and batted her eyes.

The fact that he didn't bother stopping to deliver a flirty line meant he truly did have an emergency situation to get to. In the past I'd gotten a little hurt that he didn't tell me much about his personal life when I constantly divulged too much. I also sent him way too many pictures of my cat doing funny things, but what can I say? Einstein's freaking adorable.

But I digress.

I now knew that being tight-lipped about himself was just part of who Beck was, and that was okay. Still, I couldn't help but worry. Occasionally he got this faraway look that said he had a lot on his mind, more than hockey and classes. Or maybe I was overanalyzing—as he pointed out—I tended to do that sometimes.

Which was why I was going to buy the clothes I thought were far too revealing. I'd get a couple of pairs of jeans, too. It's not like I never wore pants, but after my life-long fight with jeans that were too long, not to mention the struggle to find ones that also fit my hips, it was just easier to go with dresses, skirts, or funky leggings.

Suddenly it hit me that what I wore was more function and styles being pushed on me for the sake of not "showing off too much" than items I'd picked out myself. I'd just gotten used to them. Used to not rocking the boat. I looked at myself in the mirror, studying the outfit I was wearing. Did I even *like* my style?

Guess it doesn't matter, since I'm trying out a whole new

look anyway.

After I browsed through several more stores and racked up enough purchases to make me fear the day my credit card bill arrived, I hesitated in front of the salon. I had a few pictures on my phone, and I figured I could ask one of the hairdressers for help choosing the exact cut and style. I'd considered short and choppy, but I wasn't quite ready to lose a few feet of hair—I was planning on wearing it down more, but I still needed bun capabilities. It drove me crazy when it was in my face as I studied, and there were plenty of bold choices that didn't require me going short.

Luckily, one of the hairdressers had an opening. She ushered me into a chair, I showed her a picture, and then explained that I also wanted to do a bright, edgy color, but I couldn't decide between really blond or really dark.

She pursed her lips as she studied my hair and then my face, and then my hair again. "Blond is so harsh and hard to keep up, and with your pale skin tone, I think dark might look Gothic." She glanced over my clothes. "Which doesn't really seem like you."

"No, not the look I'm going for. But I also want edgier than my current style—I'm looking for a more modern upgrade all around."

She picked up a strand of my hair, studied it for a couple of seconds, and then asked, "Have you ever thought about going red?"

• • •

Einstein jumped onto my lap as I typed the list items I had into a document. He curled into a fluffy ball and purred as

I scratched under his chin and ran my hand down his back. Even though I was a hardcore chemistry nerd, I occasionally dabbled in physics, and when I saw my new kitty, his long gray and white hair sticking out at all angles, I knew Einstein was his name, no question about it.

I saved what I'd written so far as "College Bucket List," and then added a number four to the bottom.

So, what else should I add? In general, I was trying to be bolder and not have too many rules, but I knew myself well enough to know that I'd need certain goals to check off—I worked best that way. Little goals got me to big goals, and anything I took the time to put on paper got done. Plus, it'd keep me on schedule so I could accomplish the list by the end of this semester and go home an entirely new, more-fun and less-scared person.

I do need to make sure to keep my grades up, despite going out more.

But that didn't belong on my bucket list. Just in general life goals, and it wasn't something I'd accidentally forget to do. To get more ideas, I pulled up Google, typed "college bucket list," and started scrolling through the resulting links.

Yikes. There were a lot of things I didn't want to do. Skydive, bungee jump. Get into a bar fight, and then get thrown out. Considering my non-existent fighting skills, I'd have to be carried out on a stretcher. No thanks.

Streaking—yeah, I'd never be able to do that one. The risqué wardrobe choices I'd made earlier in the mall were enough to give me heart palpitations. Not to mention a big part of the reason I'd chosen to live in an apartment instead of the dorms was having my own private shower and bathroom—well, a bathroom with a locking door that I only had to share with one other girl—so that I didn't have to risk ever being even semi-naked in front of people I didn't know.

The other reason was Einstein. Dorms didn't allow cats, and I didn't trust my parents enough to leave him behind. Not that they wouldn't have *tried* to take care of him, but with Mom's job as a flight attendant constantly taking her away from home and Dad working all day at the coffee shop he owned in Utica, New York, no one would be there to make sure my kitty got enough love and attention—and a full food bowl.

I scratched Einstein behind his ears. I would've missed him like crazy, too. Whenever I was having a lonely day, he made me feel loved, even if only for my ability to get him food and make him comfy.

Let's see. What other suggestions do they have? I skimmed down the page to the next item. *Skip a class to have sex.*

I stared at that one. Sounded kind of exciting. Then again, why couldn't you just have sex at a normal time and not skip class? I'd never be able to focus, and wouldn't everyone else be in class around that time? Except for slacker guys, who'd never been my type.

Plus, here's the thing about sex: I didn't really get the big allure. It's not awful, but it's just okay for me. Nothing worth skipping class for and then stressing out about how to make up the work. But maybe that was me not being bold or edgy enough, and it was something I should work on.

Deciding I'd chosen a list that might be over my head—and noticing most of the items were geared toward guys, what with the "get a chick to eat a banana during a wet T-shirt contest," which was definitely against my feminist values—I clicked back and went to one of the other search options.

"Thank your favorite professor? Really?" Talk about the opposite of bold. That was just common courtesy. Then again, at least I was unknowingly doing something right already.

Try food on campus that you've never tried before.

Okay, this one's too weak. It's what I've already been doing, and by their definition of bucket list, I'm a total rebel.

Another search showed things I couldn't afford to do, like go to Hawaii and study abroad—I mean, who *didn't* want to do those things? Awesome ideas, webpage, but first I'd need to win the lottery, and I'd spent too much time studying statistics to believe that'd ever happen. As Miles used to say, the lottery was just a tax on people who weren't good at math.

I smiled at the memory of the first time he'd said it and I'd laughed, linking my fingers with his and thinking my boyfriend was smart and my kind of funny. *Man, I miss him sometimes.*

I shook my head. *Focus, Lyla.*

And then, like Goldilocks—or whatever the redheaded version of that was—I stumbled upon a list with items that were just right. The top suggestion took my number four spot.

4. Sing karaoke

I'd always wanted to do it, and had actually gone to a birthday party where they had a karaoke machine, but had chickened out. Beck was probably going to try to resist being the other half of my duet, but I'd feel much better with someone else than going solo, so I'd find a way to talk him into it.

Hmm, kiss a beautiful stranger is pretty much the same as my number three. Only that one sounds more poetic. Maybe I'll change it to that.

Oh, dancing on a bar! That one might be a good one.

Or it might be humiliating.

But I'd already ruled out skipping class to have sex, and I needed to stop talking myself out of things and go for a few of them. So I added number five, with a sub goal, of course.

5. Dance on a bar. (Learn how to sexy dance, so I don't make a fool of myself when the bar dancing happens.)

After a few more minutes, I added another one that had always appealed to me, but I'd never thought I could do.

6. Get a tattoo

It'd be something cute and feminine. Not too big, and something not many people saw. But it was definitely bold, so go me!

I skimmed the other items on the webpage, wondering if I should add anything more, but the knock at the door cut my search short. I quickly minimized my list.

Whitney stuck her head in my room. "Hey, I was wondering—whoa! Your hair!"

I shook out the thick fringe bangs and tugged one of the fiery strands in front of my face. The bright color still caught me off guard, but it also gave me a thrill every time I saw it. "What do you think?"

"It's effing fabulous. It looks amazing with your skin tone, and those bangs and the long layers really add volume and style. I'm impressed. That took balls."

My grin was probably way bigger than the situation allowed, but I did something bold. Me. Who knew I'd be so happy to be accused of having balls? "Thanks."

"A group of us are going to grab food and then go bowling. Do you wanna come with?"

I bit my lip. "Is Colin going to be there?"

"Yeah. What happened with him the other night, anyway?"

I was too embarrassed to relay what the guy had said about me, especially to the flawlessly put together girl who wore outfits Barbie would be proud to rock and looked like she belonged in a sorority house. Since Kristen was in one, I was surprised Whitney wasn't, actually. "I just don't think he and I are a good fit. I'm going to pass tonight, but I swear I'm going to go out more." Just not anywhere Colin was. There was bold, and then there was putting myself in a situation that'd destroy my limited confidence. That was the last thing I needed if I was going to go to a party in a couple of days.

Whitney leaned her hip against my doorframe, crossing one ankle over the other. "You know you can hang out with me and Kristen anytime you want, right? It makes me sad to think of you all by yourself studying while we're out."

That made me feel a bit like her pity project—she was a nice girl, her heart in the right place, but we didn't have much in common. I'd met her through the roommate finder search on the Boston College housing site. She'd fit the two requirements I needed most. 1) She didn't mind a cat, and 2) The rent she'd listed for the apartment was in my price range. Five months of living together and I still didn't know much about her besides she went out a lot, and liked guys, and that the feeling was mutual. She could probably teach me a lot about confidence and flirting, but again, if I had to deal with Colin on outings, it wasn't worth it.

"Don't worry about me. I've got Einstein to keep me company tonight." I patted his head and he snuggled his nose deeper into my sweater. "And like I said, I have plans this weekend—Beck and I are going to a party."

"Beck. Good choice." Whitney got a dreamy look on her face, no doubt picturing him now. He'd only been here a handful of times, mostly to pick me up—he was allergic to Einstein, so he could never stay long. But that was all it took for my roommate to crush on him. As soon as I suspected he might not be totally uninterested in Whitney's come-ons, I'd asked him if he could please refrain from sleeping with her. I didn't need the extra drama, and he had a ton of other options, so I didn't think it was an unfair request.

But the way Whitney said his name made me wonder if I was being unfair to her. *No, I'm saving her the hump and dump treatment. Plus she's been with what's-his-face a lot over the past few weeks, and even if that doesn't work out, it's not like she's ever had any shortage of male attention.*

And maybe, just maybe, there was a part of me that wanted Beck to myself. Not the way she wanted him, but the part I could have. He was my friend—the person I relied on out here in Boston—and if he was suddenly more interested in sleeping with my roommate than hanging out with me, it'd crush me. Especially if she became the one he decided to stick with for a while.

I didn't want to evaluate what exactly that said about

me.

"Well, see you later, then," Whitney said. Since Beck was on my mind now, I sent him a quick text checking in.

Me: *Thanks again for everything. I hope that you know I'm always here for you, whatever you need.*

After about a minute, I received a text back.

Beck: *I know*

A few seconds later, a smiley face came through, and I had to laugh. A week or so ago, I'd told him that his texts were always so short and blunt. "Couldn't you add a smiley face or something?" I'd asked.

He actually listened! A smug sense of victory swirled through me. He could be so stubborn about things that I could hardly believe it, even as the emoticon smiled up at me.

After debating just leaving it alone, I couldn't help myself. I went ahead and sent him back a winky smiley face with a nose. Excitement over our upcoming weekend plans sent sparks of energy dancing across my skin. A party. With Beck. The potential and hope morphed into an all-consuming anticipation that promised this weekend would be the one to change everything.

Chapter Six

I shook my head but couldn't help smiling about as big as the face Lyla had sent me. It'd been a long, crappy day, what with having to drive over an hour to pick up my little felon sister in New Hampshire. She'd talked to me on the phone like everything was cool, and then added, "So, uh, I'm sorta in jail right now, and I need you to bail me out."

Ever since our parents died, Megan had decided the best thing to do was get into trouble all the time and make my aunt question why she ever agreed to custody. This time it was shoplifting, which was just beyond dumb. The girl had plenty of money and a large trust fund coming to her when she turned eighteen in two years. Not to mention everything she could ever ask for at her fingertips. But she craved adventure.

Of course that made me think of Lyla and her list. I told

myself her thing was harmless, but how did one go from straight A student to total mess? Apparently my sister was hell-bent on finding out.

Aunt Tessa was still yelling, but she was starting to lose her voice, so the lecture would be wrapping up soon. Megan sat on the couch, a sullen and not nearly repentant-enough expression in place. I leaned against the archway of the living room, waiting for the grand finale.

"…just don't know what to do with you anymore. You're grounded. And we're talking no car, no phone, no TV, no going *anywhere*, grounded." Aunt Tessa stormed past me, shaking her head and muttering under her breath.

Megan threw her head back and gave a half-growl, half-sigh. Then she turned the pale blue eyes both she and I got from Mom on me. "Can I *please* come live with you?"

"What do you think?"

"Come on, I'd be good." She batted her eyes. "And you've got an extra bedroom."

I crossed the room and sat next to her on what she and I referred to as the "floral headache" couch. Aunt Tessa was so proud that it'd come from France, despite the fact that it was overly floral, so silky it practically kicked you off when you sat down, and had unforgiving trim across the top that would jab you in the skull if you tried to sit back too far. "You can't act like this, Megan. And I don't have time to keep driving up."

Her shoulders slumped, every ounce of her fiery energy draining out of her. "It's not fair. You got to escape. You don't have to drive past the old house, or deal with people constantly asking how you're adjusting. Or spreading rumors. At least now I've given them something else to talk about."

I rubbed my forehead, trying to come up with something to say to that. People talking about her getting arrested was the *last* thing our family needed. "I thought things would've calmed down by now."

"Not now that everyone knows Mom was screwing Mr. Brooks—I don't know how it got out. Not that it really matters. It's out there, so if it's not pity, it's snide remarks about her affair."

And the bombs just kept dropping and blowing up in my face. I couldn't say I didn't understand the need to escape, because it was what I'd done. What I'd wanted to do since I was fifteen and found out about my mom's affair.

"Mr. Brooks is old news," I said. "The people around here are just bored gossips reaching for scraps because they have nothing else to do. It'll fade."

"Whatever. It all blows and I'm over it." Megan stood and ran her fake nails through her perfectly highlighted hair. A year ago, she was so sweet, and now she looked like the mean girls who used to pick on her. I hated it, but the one time I'd brought it up, she'd cried and told me life was harder for girls and I just didn't get it, so I was never going there again. "Thanks for bailing me out. Just go back to college and forget about me."

I rolled my eyes. "I didn't realize you were taking drama classes this semester."

"I'm not—hey." She shoved me, but then she smiled, a hint of how things used to be breaking through. "You're right. *You* don't deserve the hate." She threw her arms around me. "I'm going to go crazy here, Beckett. Are you sure you can't take me with you?"

Yeah, the last thing I needed was to worry about my

sixteen-year-old sister surrounded by college boys, getting into even more trouble. She hadn't been nearly this upset when I'd left for freshman year. Of course, then, she hadn't had to deal with life without Mom and Dad. "I'm sorry, but you know that'd never work. Just ignore the rumors and try to keep yourself out of trouble. Before long, you'll be the one in college, and none of this gossip will matter anymore. And if you need me, you know I'm only a phone call away."

"I know." She tightened the hug. "Love ya, big brother."

I ruffled her hair. "Love you, too. But if you steal something again, I'm leaving your ass in jail."

• • •

Megan was right. There was something about driving past the old house, its large Victorian columns and sprawling lawn behind the wrought iron gate with the gilded D in the middle, that made everything inside me go cold. The money alone would've made people talk, but being part of one of the most influential families in the upper class suburb of Concord wasn't all it was cracked up to be.

Just mentioning the last name Davenport meant people automatically treated you better, but they also watched every move and gossiped about every misstep. I wasn't going to say the perks hadn't been nice most of the time, but living under the microscope nonstop wasn't easy.

I knew it'd created quite the scandal when Dad, the heir to the Davenport company and the fortune that came with it, married a girl from the wrong side of the tracks. As little kids, Megan and I had repeatedly heard the story from Mom about how, despite the odds, love conquered all.

But when I'd walked in on Mom and one of Dad's financial advisers in a compromising position—mostly clothed, thank the Lord, but still—I'd realized love wasn't as powerful as I'd once thought. Not to mention the whole scarred-for-life thing. Even worse, Mom continued to act completely in love with Dad, not a single slipup. Every time she'd call to say she had meetings for her various charities, I wondered if she was lying. It was such a relief when I found out she'd told Dad about the affair. Harboring a secret from the guy I'd admired most in the world had eaten away at me.

They'd gone to counseling to repair their marriage, and there at the end, everything seemed to be working. They'd still had their problems, but they always put on a united front. I'd hoped it was because things were okay, but maybe it was just for the sake of the company.

She swore she'd ended it. Surely it hadn't still been going on.

Whether it was old news that'd surfaced, or if Mom had slipped off the fidelity wagon, it was out there for the entire town to discuss and analyze now. As if losing both parents in one fell swoop wasn't a hard enough blow for our family and hadn't caused enough talk. It was why I loved my anonymity at college—I'd decided to leave my showier, chromed-out Escalade in favor of the older Land Rover, and with the exception of having my own apartment, I worked to hide the fact that I had money.

Not just money, I had responsibility that'd only get worse in less than a year. Control of the company was due to transfer to me on my twenty-first birthday, because apparently that was old enough to suddenly be in charge of a large pharmaceutical company that employed thousands of people.

No pressure.

Dad had always pushed me toward the sciences, and I liked them well enough, but I'd need a stronger business base to successfully run the company. Dad loved the company as much as his father had, and his father before that. It was in our blood, he used to say. After my first year at college, he took me aside and told me I needed to take more serious classes to get ready for a future position at D&T Pharmaceuticals. Neither of us had known at the time just how soon that'd need to happen.

Mom always reassured me I didn't have to go into the family company if I didn't want to—that she'd still be proud, as long as I didn't turn into a spoiled rich jerk. When I'd wanted to play hockey over polo—which was the norm for the sons in my parents' circle of friends—she'd helped me talk Dad into letting me go out for the rougher sport.

Hockey was one thing, but she'd known as well as I had that Dad would've been disappointed if I decided to take another career path. The people at the company were going to expect me to do something to pull my weight and keep getting paid, and with Megan relying on me, too, I wondered if I should quit the hockey team and focus on getting through college faster.

Just the thought of no hockey made everything I tried to keep at bay press in on me. There were a few weeks at the beginning of summer that I barely remembered, just a blur of grief and crying and the funeral, and thinking my parents being gone had to be a bad dream. There were still bad days here and there, but once I'd gotten back to Boston, it felt like I could breathe again, and a big part of that was getting on the ice.

Four colleges had given me the red-carpet treatment, but Boston College had one of the best hockey programs in the nation, and it was the entire reason I'd chosen to go there. The location—close enough to go home when I needed to and also near where the Bruins played—was just icing on the cake.

Scouts from the Bruins occasionally attended the BC games, and would of course be at playoff games, and my main focus for the past year and a half had been getting good enough for them to notice me before I graduated. I'd hoped getting drafted would give me a chance to delay working with Dad for a few more years and play for the NHL. A long shot, but it was what I'd dreamed about ever since the first time I gripped a hockey stick.

I needed to face the fact that that dream was gone now and shift my focus to taking over the family business and running the company in a way that would've made Dad proud. To making sure Megan had the stable future she was obviously craving.

For the rest of the season I'd give hockey everything I had and go out as high as possible—NCAA championship would be the ultimate way to achieve that, and our team had a good shot at the title. Then, when the season ended—no doubt it'd feel way too soon when it came—I'd trade my hockey stick and skates for suits and ties and at least have the glory days to relive when I was bored out of my mind.

Sorrow rose up, and I accelerated out of town, wanting to put this place behind me while I could.

Let's see, what day is it?

Wednesday. That meant hockey and classes to keep me

busy the next few days, then the party with Lyla. Followed by our low-key Sunday movie night—that was the part of the week I was most looking forward to. Those were the nights I was just a regular guy hanging out with a not-so-regular girl, with little to no effort required to keep the depressing thoughts constantly spinning through my head at bay.

Chapter Seven

Lyla

Nerd is such a broad term when you think about it. Or maybe I liked thinking about it that way, because it meant I didn't fit into a box. But seriously, there were science fiction nerds, there were the socially awkward nerds, people who role-played and were into comic books, guys and girls who could work wonders with technology, and then there were the because-you're-smart nerds.

Okay, so I definitely had some overlap going on, but technology tended to do the opposite of what I wanted it to, and I'd never gotten into comic books or role-playing games. Science fiction wasn't my thing, either. Funny, because I was fairly obsessed with chemistry which was, you know, a science. It's not like I was opposed to science fiction—I'd seen the odd movie or read a book here and there that was interesting enough—but I didn't have the commitment to be a Trekkie or a Whovian or whatever other subset was out there.

As I was pulling on my new outfit in my room, legs freshly shaven and coated in shimmery lotion, I decided I was in the because-I-am-smart-and-socially-awkward category of nerd. The smartness came from a lot of hard work, though—a plethora of nights spent studying like crazy so I could get a scholarship, because it was the only way I could afford college, as my parents had reminded me often. I think the obsession with good grades, combined with lack of sunlight and interactions with the general population, might've messed with my social skills.

You would've thought Mom's Mexican genes would've at least given me an eternal tan, but nope. With this outfit, it would've been especially nice, considering all the skin I had on display. The hips she gave me were definitely in full force, though, and I was doing my best to shut out the horrified comments and looks I'd get if she saw me showing off my curves in a getup like this. On top of that, my heart was beating way too fast, my previous anticipation and high hopes had dissolved, and I was now fairly certain this night was destined to end in me making a fool of myself.

The few high school parties I'd attended with Miles had been relatively quiet—we never knew about the loud, pack-three-hundred-people-in-a-house ones until we showed up at school on Monday and heard how "killer" they were. He didn't drink, so I'd decided not to out of solidarity, and the fact that my parents would've freaked if they found out. It'd just gotten to be a habit somewhere along the way, I supposed. Since I'd started college, I'd tried a few drinks here and there, but I always kept myself in control.

No more. Not tonight, anyway.

Whitney poked her head in. "You ready for me?"

"Yeah. Thanks again for helping me." First step of letting go a little was recruiting my roommate to do my makeup. I'd watched a few tutorials, figuring I was nothing if not a fast learner, but my technique still needed work, and tonight was too important to mess up.

"Anytime." Whitney sat across from me, took out her makeup brushes, and got to work swiping liquids and powders across my skin, hopefully taking away the last traces of the girl who was too afraid to let loose. "You've got great cheekbones, and just wait until I get done with your eyes. They're totes gonna pop."

I wrinkled my nose. "That sounds oozy."

She laughed and directed me to look up. As she swiped the mascara wand across my lashes, I asked, "How was bowling the other night? Are you and Matt a thing now?"

Whitney sighed and returned the mascara wand to its tube. "We haven't had *the talk* about our relationship. Like I'm hoping that he's only dating me, but I don't want to be the girl who asks, because guys always read it as needy or too serious, and I don't want to mess things up, you know?"

No, I didn't really know. The bottom of my stomach dropped out. Having a steady boyfriend through most of high school hadn't prepared me for all these new college dating rules. If Whitney thought she was going to mess things up, I was going to do nuclear damage when I tried.

Good thing I'm not looking for anything serious right now. Hopefully there are fewer rules involved with being flirty and free.

Whitney applied lipstick to my lips, then handed me

a tissue and instructed me to kiss it. She then slicked on another smooth layer that smelled like bubble gum before sitting back, a satisfied expression on her face. "You look amazing. Take a peek."

I stood and opened my closet door. The girl in the mirror with the dressy black shorts—to keep from flashing everyone in case of keg stand—and purple, low-cut top that complimented her new fiery hair color was bold. Fearless. Her makeup was flawless, with shiny nude-colored lips, shimmery silver lids, and black cat-eye liner that did, in fact, make her eyes pop. Even better, she didn't look like *any* kind of nerd.

"Wow, Whit. You do good work."

Whitney's reflection showed up next to mine, a big smile stretched across her lips. "It's easy when I've got a pretty canvas to work with."

Warmth filled my chest. I didn't have any close girl-friends, so maybe that's why I didn't realize she was one till now. I turned and hugged her, and she squeezed me back.

"Good luck tonight," Whitney said. "Have fun. Meet lots of hot guys. Tell me all about it tomorrow."

"I will. Unless you wanna come?"

"Nah, I've got plans with Matt. If he's with me every night that means he's not dating anyone else, right?"

"Sounds like a logical conclusion to me."

She gave me a hope-filled smile and then gathered up her makeup and left my room. Beck texted to say he was in the parking lot as I was adding another spritz of perfume, and I moved over to my desk to close my laptop. I hesitated, reading my first few list items.

Maybe I'll save the making out with a beautiful stranger

for later. Of course, the drinking would probably help the nerves bouncing around in my stomach. I hoped. And I probably wouldn't look this pretty ever again, not to mention my timetable got shorter by the day, and I planned on adding a few more things to the list before I'd feel like it was complete. *Okay, I'll do it tonight.*

I took a deep breath to combat the anxiety gnawing my insides, stepped into black strappy heels that were sexy but not so easy to walk in, and paused at my doorway.

Was I really going to go somewhere dressed like this? I fought my instinct to look down and think about how much skin I was currently exposing and told myself once again that I could be bold. I could party with reckless abandon the way the rest of my peers did.

No letting fear get the best of you. Remember, rapid changes take catalysts.

I lifted my chin and made my way downstairs, careful not to step on the left side of the stairs where the ice rarely melted since it was forever in shade. My palms were so sweaty by the time I got to Beck's Land Rover that it took me two tries to open the door—so the sexy was already happening.

I slid into the passenger seat and turned to Beck, waiting for him to laugh at me and tell me to go change. His attention was on his phone, though, the brim of his black and yellow Bruins cap blocking my view of his face. But then he finally glanced over at me.

And did a double take.

My face flushed as he ran his gaze down my body and all the way back up. "Damn, Lyla. That's what you've been hiding under those scarves and long skirts?"

I shrugged, because how else do you respond to a

question like that? I reached down and messed with the ankle strap of my shoes. "Is it okay, then? I feel…naked." When he didn't say anything, I turned my face toward him, shaking my bangs out of my eyes.

Beck shifted into reverse and backed out of the parking spot. "You're good. And I like the hair."

Good? Like *the hair?* Those words seemed so mediocre, especially compared to how I felt. My bangs fell in my eyes again and I swept them away, fighting the urge to gather the rest of my hair into a bun. "Please tell me it's at least an improvement."

Beck slowed the SUV, stopping just short of exiting the parking lot. Then he turned his eyes on me—were they darker than usual? I swore they were, but it must've been a trick of the light. He swallowed, his Adam's apple bobbing up and down, and there was something mesmerizing about the motion.

"You look so different, it was hard to believe it was even you at first," he said. "I feel like saying that you look better is an insult to how you usually look, but I'll admit the red hair is sexy as hell, and your legs and your…" His gaze dipped to my cleavage, and I fought the urge to cover it up. Maybe I should've brought, like, a tiny scarf. Just a little something. "If you're asking if guys will notice you at this party, the answer is yes. Trust me on that."

There was an edge to his voice I hadn't heard before and it sent an unexpected dart of heat through me. I tried to swallow, but it wasn't really working, so I settled for nodding. *Relax. He's just complimenting your new look, and you desperately needed the reassurance—that's it.*

Beck turned up the music, and we didn't talk much on

the way to the Quad. When we got there, he squeezed into a narrow gap at the end of a packed parking lot that I wasn't even sure was legal, unhooked his seatbelt, and turned to me. "If you change your mind about this, or decide you're over the party at any time, just let me know. And I know you want to let loose, but there are guys out there who'll try to take advantage. That's why, with every drink you have, the closer I'll be. Try not to puke *on* me, okay?"

"Ew. I know the other night I said that was the goal, but stop me before I get quite that far. Deal?"

"Deal."

Beck met me at the back of the Land Rover and we wove in and out of cars toward the large squat building with a line of people streaming into it. The bass from the music boomed out, so loud the beats echoed under my skin. I wanted so badly not to be nervous—to believe my new look was all it took to take on the party crowd—but my frayed nerves weren't convinced. If anything, they were unraveling faster and faster with each step closer to the front door.

An icy breeze hit me and I shivered—another con for wearing so little clothing.

Beck placed his hand on the small of my back, the contact calming my nerves and the heat from his touch taking the edge off the cold. With the shoes on, I was three inches taller than usual, but he still had several inches on me. The added height gave me a closer view of the blond scruff dusting his strong jawline, though.

By the time we reached the door, even the fact that Beck's hand remained on my back didn't stop my stomach from tying itself in knots again. My thoughts turned to how relaxing a night on the couch in my comfy clothes would have been. A movie or a book required no panicking about what to do or say. No wondering how far I'd bend before accidentally flashing someone.

"Your college party experience awaits," Beck said. Then he studied me, no doubt seeing the worry etched across my features. "Unless you've changed your mind."

I took a deep breath, the frigid air burning my throat on the way down, then squared my shoulders. "Nope. I'm doing this. Just, uh, stay close. Okay?"

"Sure thing."

The music grew even louder as we stepped inside, and the buzz of simultaneous conversations mixed in. People crowded the center of the space, dancing to the beat. Pairs, large groups, smaller groups, the wallflowers—they were all here, spread throughout the room.

"Lyla?"

I pulled my attention off the gyrating bodies and turned to Beck, who was gesturing me in the other direction. My ankle wobbled slightly, and I inwardly cursed the heels. Careful of where I stepped, I followed Beck's familiar hat through the crowd. There was a large table in the corner covered in alcohol.

Beck put his hand on my back again, and leaned in close, talking loud to be heard over the music. "You ever have beer before?"

"Yeah. It's pretty gross, but I've been assured it's an acquired taste."

"Hang tight. We'll start with something that tastes better and will get you buzzed fast, and then we'll work up to the keg stand."

The smile, combined with the hand on my back and a

whiff of his cologne sent a flutter through my stomach.

What the what? First the strange reaction in the car, then thinking about his eyes and his scruff, and now I'm getting butterflies? Don't go doing that to me, body.

"Sounds good." Clearly, my senses were in overdrive or something. As I watched Beck move over to the table, I tried to think if he'd ever touched me so often before.

No, because we're usually sitting on his couch eating ice cream and watching movies. And before that we mostly studied. But he usually opens doors for me when we go places. Maybe I'd just always worn too many clothes to notice his hand on my back. Either way, I knew better than to get flutters over Beck Davenport. The guy had longer relationships with cereal boxes than girls, and I wouldn't even be on his radar in that area, looking for only temporary fun or not. We were just two chemistry nerds who'd built a friendship out of our mutual love of effortless hangouts involving movies and food—he was a closet nerd, whereas I let my love of science hang out there for the world to see.

But not tonight.

"Hey," a guy near me said, and I looked to my right and then my left. There wasn't anyone else super close by, and the few who were near us were involved in other conversations.

"Me?" I asked, still not quite trusting he was talking to me.

One corner of his mouth kicked up. "Yeah, you. I'm CJ. I saw you across the room and had to come and say hi."

"Oh. Thanks. Cool. Lyla. That's my name."

He seemed to be waiting for something else, and I kicked myself for not looking up good party conversation starters. Finding it hard to meet his steady gaze, I glanced down and noticed some gray and white cat hair on my shirt. I wiped at it. "Sorry. My cat, Einstein, always sheds. Not that I'm a crazy cat lady or anything. I've just got the one. I mean, I had two when I was in junior high, but they both died. Not at the same time, or that would've been awful. It was still pretty sad. But now I have Einstein, and he's super mellow, not to mention, like, the cutest cat ever."

CJ nodded awkwardly, and I knew I should've stuck with keeping my mouth shut. After another weird beat where he just blinked at me, he walked away. Beck was standing off to the side, two red plastic cups in hand.

"Dead cats? You said you had a hard time talking to guys, but shit, Debbie Downer, I had no idea."

My spirits sagged, taking my confidence along with them.

"Don't worry." Beck held out a cup to me. "The good thing about parties is there's always another opportunity waiting around the corner. But let's get you loosened up a bit before we try again."

I took a generous gulp from the cup. Coke with a hint of coconut—much yummier than beer. Then I eyed the cup in his hand. "What about driving later?"

"It's just Coke. Don't worry about me, I'm the responsible one tonight. You're the one who doesn't worry about things, remember?" Beck stepped aside for a couple weaving through the crowd and then took my elbow and pulled me away from the steady stream of traffic headed toward the drink table.

"Here's a tip," he said. "When a guy comes up to you, ask him questions. Keep reflecting the conversation back to him. People love talking about themselves. Asking about their major might be overdone, but it'll get the conversation going. Music. Hobbies. Things like that. And then, if the guy seems into the conversation, move a little closer—it's loud in here, so you've got the perfect excuse." He set his cup on a nearby ledge. "Try it out on me."

"Do I have to? I'll feel stupid. Plus, I already know you."

Beck crossed his arms and looked down at me, all intimidation. I tipped back my drink, stalling for time, but he patiently waited, still staring me down when I finally lowered the cup from my lips.

"Fine, Coach. But just to be clear, I'm not going to drop and give you twenty if I mess up." Going off the flirting I'd seen Whitney and Kristen do, I flipped my hair and shot him what I hoped was a sexy grin but felt like it might land me more on the possibly-a-psycho scale. "Beck, was it? So, like, what do you do for fun?"

His lips twitched and as I waited for his response, I was already trying to figure out what I should say next. But then his ridiculously blue eyes focused on me and only me, my breath caught, and suddenly my main thought was, *Pretend flirting or not, no matter what you do, do* not *comment on his eyes or the way they're currently sending a shiver of electricity up your spine.*

Chapter Eight

Telling myself I shouldn't be staring at Lyla's boobs wasn't working as well as it should've, the same way it hadn't when she'd first gotten in my car tonight. And when I tried to look away from them, there were her shapely legs peeking out of those tiny shorts to distract me. When she said she was going for a new look, I figured it'd be a trim that I'd get in trouble for not noticing, and maybe a new outfit. I had to hand it to her, though, she'd really gone all out.

The feisty redhead in front of me looked completely opposite of the girl who usually sat cross-legged on my couch, her skirt spread out like a blanket as she commented on every unbelievable part of the movie that she "just didn't buy." But the train-wreck conversation I'd witnessed a minute ago proved that girl was still in there. Which was why I needed to *not* say, "Girls like you," the way my instincts automatically told me to. That was a line for a very different type of girl.

So instead I went for a less bold response that'd help her work on her social skills. "I play hockey. I'm on the college team, actually."

She licked her lips—another feature of hers I most definitely shouldn't stare at—and then she shook her head, almost as if she'd been somewhere else for a moment. "Cool. I've never been to a hockey game."

"You should come to one. Watch me play." It was typical conversation, just like we'd talked about, but I wondered why she'd never come to a game. It'd be nice to have her there cheering me on, but judging from the way she constantly flinched during fight scenes in movies, she'd probably think it was too violent.

"I'll have to check my schedule," she said with another hair flip.

Now she was getting it, although she needed to learn another move—we'd go into that later. Right now she needed a confidence boost. "So, Lyla, what's your major?"

She tilted her head and sighed.

"Let's try a little less attitude. We don't want the guys thinking you're stuck-up."

"Jerk," she muttered, shoving my chest, and I laughed.

"Come on, you talk to me all the time, and you're perfectly normal. Funny and passionate, with no trouble putting me in my place." I took a sip of my soda, looking at her over the rim so she'd know she might as well answer, because I wouldn't budge until she did.

She ran her hand through her hair, the new bright-hued bangs immediately falling back over one eye. "The 'normal' part is debatable, and it doesn't count because it's you, and I'm not trying to impress you. When I talk to a cute guy, my brain says be cool, but my mouth says screw you, brain, and then stupid things come out. I don't think I can practice it away."

"Not with that attitude, you can't," I said. A girl carrying a tray full of Jell-O shots walked by, and I snagged two. "Here. You're drinking too slow."

After Lyla took care of the shots, making a sour face after each one, we picked up with the typical party small talk, and I went back into instructor mode.

"Now, act like you didn't hear what I said, put your hand on my massive bicep" —I flashed her a teasing smile, hoping it'd help put her at ease—"then lean in and say, 'Huh?' And make sure you sound as ditzy as possible."

The wheels were turning as she psyched herself up to make the move, which was funny considering we were only practicing. Finally, she put her hand on my arm, leaned in so close her warmth soaked into me and I could smell the cherry Jell-O shots on her breath as she said, "Huh?" Then she bit her lip. It was a nervous tick she had, but in this instance, it totally worked for her.

"See," I said, finding myself staring into her eyes and thinking that they were bigger and brighter than usual. My heart gave one hard pump that sent a burst of adrenaline through my veins. I cleared my throat, trying to get my thoughts back on track. "That wasn't so hard, was it?"

Lyla stepped back, and an unanticipated twinge of disappointment over the space suddenly between us twisted my chest. My dry spell must be messing with my head.

A couple of girls wearing even less than Lyla walked by,

giggling and wobbling enough it was clear they were already past tipsy.

"If you wanna experiment," I said, "I hear college is a good time for girls to kiss girls. I'll supervise."

Lyla smacked my chest, harder than she'd ever done before. "Don't be pervy."

I laughed, rubbing the spot she'd hit as if I were really injured. "If you're doing this experiment, there's something you should know. All guys are pervy. Some just hide it better than others."

She frowned at me. "All guys?"

The disappointment in her voice almost caused me to take it back. But she should know what she was getting herself into. I saw how hurt she was when her boring dud of a boyfriend broke up with her—it'd be way too easy for some player jackass to use her and leave her crushed.

Even though I told myself not to soften it, I found myself saying, "You've got your complete assholes, and then there are the guys who are actually good guys and do their best to be decent. You want to go for the nicer pervs."

The dimple in her cheek showed up as a smile broke free.

I cupped her elbow, and okay, I might've accidentally on purpose brushed my thumb across her soft skin. "Buzzed enough to try a keg stand?"

She glanced over to where people were filling their cups up from the tap. "No one else is doing one, though. Wouldn't it be weird if I did it now? And you know, won't people be a little grossed out afterward that my germs are on the—"

I slid my hand down to hers and tugged her toward the keg. "Trust me, people won't care, and within a few minutes, I guarantee there will be at least a couple of guys circling.

Then you can try out your new moves."

If I knew she wouldn't regret backing out, I wouldn't push, but I could see that she wanted to break free for a night. Her years of being a rule follower, not to mention how she overanalyzed everything, just held her back. Once we got to the keg, it took all of two seconds to find another spotter and someone to work the tap.

I explained exactly how to do it, and Lyla's eyes went wide as she gripped the metal rim. "Ready?" I asked, but we were already hoisting her up.

The crowd counted the seconds. They got to eight before she kicked out and we set her down. She spun to the other guy, putting her hands on his arms to steady herself. At first I thought she was putting my instructions to good use, but when she stumbled back, saying, "Sorry," I realized she'd thought it was me.

I put my hand on her shoulder and slowly spun her around. "I'm here. You okay?"

She nodded.

"Want to go again?"

She shook her head. Already there were more girls lined up, ready to get the attention they so badly wanted, while Lyla was pushing away from it as fast as she could. The other guy who'd held her up obviously would've been happy to chat with her—he'd done less holding her up and more staring at her boobs.

A thread of heat stitched its way through my gut, but I worked to push it back. Lyla wanted to be seen as the hot girl. With the outfit she had on, I could hardly get pissed at every guy who ogled her like she was nothing more than a toy for them to play with.

She wobbled as we made our way from the crowd, and I caught her around the waist. I wasn't sure if she was feeling the effects of the alcohol or if it was those shoes that made her legs look so damn good. When her eyes met mine, though, she smiled. "At least I did it."

"You did."

"That beer was super disgusting, though." She wrinkled her adorable little nose. "I think the taste is going to be in my mouth forever."

"I'll go get you something else. Just Coke, or do you want rum in it again?"

"Maybe a little rum?"

"On it."

I made sure she had a wall to lean on and then headed back to the drink table. While I was there, I ran into Jeff, one of my teammates, and an all-around good guy. One of the nice pervs, I suppose, which gave me an idea.

"Hey, you see that girl over there?"

Jeff followed my pointed finger. "The redhead with the nice rack?"

That same hot pinch went through my gut, and I again told it to shut up. Lyla wanted to make out with a stranger, and who was I to stop her? I'd tried to give her the skills to draw a guy in for a longer conversation, too, but now that she was drunk? Well, who knew what she'd say? "Go take her this," I said, placing the rum and Coke in his hand, "and chat with her for a while. Even if she… Just talk to her, okay? Make sure you tell her she looks nice—leave the rack out of it."

He nodded and took a step toward her. I caught his shoulder, halting his progress. "You can kiss her if she seems interested, but that's as far as it goes. Put your hands on her and I'll make it my personal mission to ensure you limp home from practice every day."

Jeff stared at me, mouth ajar.

I shoved him forward. "What are you waiting for? Go already."

As he headed toward her, his reluctance clear, I realized I might've gone too far. With sending him. With telling him I'd hurt him if he touched her. Shit, I felt like some kind of kissing pimp now.

"Hi," a blonde breathed at me as she pushed her body against my side. Under normal circumstances, I'd make small talk. See where it led. It'd been long enough that I was tempted, but then Jeff reached Lyla, and I was watching her flash him a smile. When he first offered her the drink, she hesitated, but then Jeff gestured at me. I nodded to let her know it was from me and she took the cup from him.

Letting him talk, good… Just be cool, girl.

The blonde got offended and walked off, which reminded me that I'd never called Monica back, and that if I did, she'd yell so long it wouldn't be worth it. Cross that one off the list. She was probably too hot and cold to be even a semi-steady thing anyway. Drag it out much longer and regardless of her claim to be cool with our arrangement, she'd suddenly show up at hockey practices, thinking watching me train somehow equaled getting closer. Not only was I not interested in a relationship, I didn't have time to maintain one, keep up with classes, *and* lead my team to playoffs.

After a couple of minutes of nodding at whatever Jeff was saying, Lyla glanced around. I moved closer, waiting to see if she made any other signs she was over talking to him.

She swayed, putting her fingers to her forehead, and I realized I'd overestimated how much she could drink. From the looks of things, it was catching up to her fast.

"Hey, guys," I said. "Lyla, I see you met Jeff. He's on the hockey team with me."

He gave me a look that said I was no longer considered on his list of friends. *Jeez, be a little bitch about it, why don't you?*

"Everything's a little spinny," Lyla said with a laugh. She wobbled and clamped onto my arm. "My lips feel funny."

Jeff glanced from her to me and slowly backed away, shaking his head.

Lyla turned her big hazel eyes up to me. "I didn't say anything about my cats," she slurred. "He seemed nice, and he was talking about hockey, but then his head kinda separated in two and I decided making out with someone I don't—or kissing a beautiful stranger—or what was it again…?"

I took the red cup out of her hand—she must've been nervous because she'd already downed it. "Okay, no more drinking."

"Dancing?"

"How about we find a place to sit? You did eat tonight, didn't you?"

She tugged my arm, heading toward the section where everyone was wildly flinging themselves around, the beat forgotten with their inhibitions. "Dancing."

Considering the path my thoughts kept straying down—and that was *without* our bodies being smashed together—I couldn't think of a worse idea. But she gave another hard tug, her resolve clear.

Well, hell. Apparently, we were dancing.

Chapter Nine

LYLA

Every once in a while, I'd bump into Beck, but he'd just laugh and steady me, so I figured he didn't mind. My head felt pleasantly floaty, and I was pretty proud of the fact that I wasn't even slightly nauseous. Weirdly enough, standing still and walking were way more challenging than dancing right now. It was like the beat told my body where to go when it wasn't sure, and I was already swaying, so I just went with it. Man, I loved to dance!

Near the end of the second song, Beck gave me a funny look, the line of his jaw tight. His chest rose and then fell with a deep breath, almost like he was fortifying himself.

"What?" I asked, trying to stop swaying and totally failing until I put a hand on his arm.

He shook his head. "Nothing."

"Just tell me, I can take it." I cringed, already expecting

the worst. "I've been singing too loud, right? When I get excited, I really belt it out, which is bad, because I'm totally tone deaf."

The crooked smile he gave me eased the anxiety trying to work its way through my happy buzz. "The singing's fine. I like how you make up your own lyrics instead of singing the right ones." He put his hand on my hip, pulled me close, and hovered his lips next to my ear. My stomach crawled up to my throat and I wrapped my hand around his biceps, my thumb running across the curve there. Somewhere in the back of my mind, I knew this was a bad idea, but the other sensations were louder—racing pulse, fuzzy pleasantness, his firm body pressed against me, his hand sliding around to rest on my back. "You've got several guys checking you out, and you're wasting all your cute on me. Why don't you go circulate?"

Beck stepped back, his sudden absence a shock to my revved up body. *Other guys? Huh?*

Then I noticed two girls eye-humping him, and they didn't look like they'd mind sharing him, either. He glanced their way and then slowly back at me.

"Right. You want to meet girls." That sufficiently doused the happy from my mood. I shook my head, feeling like a moron. Stupid alcohol, glorious one moment and making you think idiotic thoughts about one of your closest friends the next. "I've gotten in your way a lot lately. I wasn't even thinking. Go, pick up a girl, or at least get a few numbers. I'll be fine on my own for a bit."

"Lyla, that's not it. It's not like I can't go without for a while." He curled his hand around the brim of his baseball cap, molding it the way he did when he needed to keep his hands busy. "I just wasn't sure if you were going to check another item off your list. Wasn't that what this party's all about?"

Sure. Check everything off now so he wouldn't have to spend every weekend plastered to my side, basically baby-sitting me. How embarrassing that I thought he was having fun, too. I worked to sound as casual as possible. "Yeah, and I definitely want to accomplish my list this semester, but…" I glanced at all the people, but between the spinning and the music and the lights, dizziness set in, tilting the floor under my feet.

Beck reached for me right as someone knocked into me from behind, and I ended up having to brace my hands on his chest. *Holy muscles, Batman. It's like hitting a wall. A warm, solid, smokin' hot wall.*

He gripped both of my arms, just above the elbow, and tingly zips of heat spread from his touch and skittered across my skin. "We can keep dancing, if that's what you want. I'm down for whatever."

I licked my lips, trying to wade through my sluggish thoughts. "No, you're right. No time like the present. When you're as behind as I am, missing an opportunity isn't an option."

Suddenly I did feel a little nauseated. I wasn't sure if it was the alcohol, or the dancing, or the weirdo attraction vibes. Maybe I just needed to be drunker. Yeah, that must be it. "I'm gonna go grab another drink. You mingle, I'll mingle. We'll meet in the middle."

"Are you sure?" he asked, his large hands still fully wrapped around my arms and making me feel things I shouldn't.

Which meant I needed to be drunker *and* put space between us before I did something stupid like try to kiss a beautiful not-stranger, who would then decide we couldn't be friends anymore. "It's a party. I appreciate you being the more responsible one, but that doesn't mean you can't have fun. See you in a bit."

With every step I took away from him, the more like myself I felt. *Wait. The point is to* not *feel like myself, though.* Thoughts weren't connecting like they should, but when a cute guy stopped me and asked me if I wanted a drink, I said sure.

We headed over to the table overflowing with alcohol, exchanging names on the way. By the end of the heavy-on-the-vodka red drink, and a conversation that was too out of focus for me to really follow, the world had blurred into nothing more than colors and sounds, reality melting away with it.

• • •

I shot up and immediately regretted it. Some little bastard was hammering away at my brain, and my mouth was a desert wasteland. It took me a moment to realize I was at Beck's.

In his bedroom.

In his *bed*.

I lifted the covers, letting out a relieved breath when I saw I still had on my clothes. Pressing my fingers to my forehead, I swung my legs over the side of the bed and screeched when the floor moved under my feet. Beck was stretched out on the carpet, a pillow under his head. He squinted up at me as his hand wrapped around my ankle.

"Please tell me I didn't puke on you," I said.

"There were a few close calls, but you didn't puke. I did

have to carry you in here, though, and then you got super chatty. When I tried to go sleep on the couch, you asked me to never leave you alone again, so…"

I dropped my head in my hands, all too aware of the weird thoughts I'd had about Beck last night. "Did I say anything embarrassing?"

"No, mostly just random stuff, heavy on the cat and science references, as usual."

I peeked through my fingers. "Did I end up making out with anyone at the party?"

"That jackass you were talking to started to pull you away from the crowd, but I cut him off. You gave him your number, but I don't think he'll be calling you after what I said to him. Sorry about that." His tone conveyed that he wasn't actually sorry at all.

Beck sat up, his hair more a mess than a stylized mess now, although he still made it look good. "You went to a party, did a keg stand, and got so drunk you forgot half the night. Congrats on this amazing milestone in your life." He squeezed my leg. "What are you gonna do next?"

"Uh, Disneyland?" I spotted a pen on his side table, so I wound my hair into a bun and secured it in place. "Actually, I'm thinking breakfast. Is that thing about greasy food being a good hangover cure true?"

"There's nothing bacon can't fix." Beck glanced at the clock. "I've got just enough time to hit the diner around the corner before I need to get going on the rest of my day. This huge assignment in econ is trying to kill me, and I want to knock it out before my game tonight."

We'd only been practicing conversation skills last night, but he'd said I should go to a game, and the more I thought about it, the more I wanted to. "Would you be embarrassed if I came to watch you play?"

The beat of silence made my stomach clench—I was blurring the lines too much. Already I had him helping me with my list, carrying me home from parties, and I didn't want to smother him.

But then a smile spread across his face. "Not at all. It'd be cool."

"Yeah?"

"Yeah. But best lay off the booze for one night. I might be too distracted to keep the guys off you."

"*Pfft*. Like that's gonna be a problem." I stepped over the piles of clothes littering the floor of his room and headed to the bathroom. My eyeliner had made a run for my cheeks, so I cleaned it up the best I could. Figured it was nice enough for the diner, at least.

All that really mattered was that, in the light of day, I was thinking clearly enough to realize that Beck was an awesome friend and nothing more. I'd never do anything to risk messing that up, either. I needed him in a way I didn't need most people.

Momentary attraction aside, I'd say last night had been a success. I'd hit a huge party and had fun, even if the last half was a bit blurred—very college, if I do say so myself. With two items checked off the list, I was feeling pretty good about life. As for finding a cute boy to make out with, there was this total hottie who always studied at the same spot in the library. I'd wanted to approach him a dozen times, but hadn't been able to work up the courage.

This afternoon, I was going to walk right up to him and put Beck's flirting tips to good use.

Chapter Ten

BECK

I was so full I could hardly move, but my giant "works" breakfast with double the pancakes was probably all I'd eat until after the game. It was already getting to be late in the day, and nothing was worse than skating on a too-full stomach. Not to mention how my gut always churned before a big game. I thought I'd get over it in time, but for about an hour leading up to every single game, I was sure I was going to puke.

Then I'd get onto the ice, adrenaline would take over, and I'd be fine. I opened the passenger door of the Land Rover for Lyla. Luckily things were back to normal between us today. It helped that she wasn't constantly knocking against me, making it impossible to not think about her curves. Last night when she'd bumped her hips into mine on the dance floor, my body had reacted in all the wrong ways.

She'd been so cute, singing the wrong lyrics as she swung her hair and bounced around. Not like I could help that it'd turned me on, and I'd kept thinking, *Any second she's going to call me on it.*

Hopefully she'd been too drunk to notice, or had blanked out that part of the night. Still, right before I closed the door, I took another look at her sexy legs. Toned thighs that led to perfectly curved calves and a whole lot of creamy soft skin.

Combine that and the fact that she had the morning-after look, was it any wonder the waiter had flashed me a thumbs-up when he took the menus from us?

"Why didn't you tell me I had syrup on my face?" Lyla asked when I settled behind the steering wheel. Her tongue darted out, licking the corner of her lip. I went to put the key in the ignition and missed.

What the hell was wrong with me? This was what I got for ignoring Monica's calls and going around half-cocked.

Finally I got the key in the right place and made it to Lyla's apartment complex. As she started out of the car, I remembered what she'd said about the game. "Wait. You want me to get you a ticket to the game?"

"Can't I get one there?"

"It's easier to get one ahead." She probably didn't know how expensive they were, either. Or where to sit. I took out my phone and pulled up the site to order tickets to the game at Kelley Rink. "I'll get it. You have ink in your printer?"

She nodded. "But you don't have t—"

"Already done." A seat next to our bench was even available. Better yet, with my attention on my phone, I could keep myself from checking out Lyla for the hundredth time. "I'll forward you the email. Just print it and bring it to the game. And if you get too busy, no worries. I know how caught up you get in studying."

"Thanks, Beck. And thanks again for last night." The grin she shot me showed off that dimple I was suddenly noticing every few seconds. Had it always been there? "See you later."

I nodded and refocused on my phone's screen. I forwarded the email with the tickets and waited until she was safely inside before heading home to study.

It only took thirty minutes to realize I was never going to ace my economics class. At this point, I'd be happy with a C. I liked my science classes, but when it came to the business ones, my brain shut down. I fought the urge to throw the textbook across the room. I imagined how satisfying the loud smack would be as it hit the wall, and even better, if it broke the spine and made the nonsense-filled pages scatter across the floor.

But then I'd have to gather them and try to put the book back together. It definitely wouldn't get me any closer to passing the class.

If I can't even get through the beginner business classes, how am I going to get through them when they get more complicated? And how am I going to take over a company when I clearly fail at comprehending the principles it's founded on?

I got supply and demand, but once you threw in graphs and analyzing data, my mind drifted to hockey plays and formations.

I closed the textbook and tossed it aside, the thump against the coffee table only mildly satisfying. For something that supposedly ran in my blood, I sure sucked at it. The blood carrying that knowledge needed to find its way to my brain, preferably sometime before I turned twenty-one.

Hopefully hands-on training will give me the skills I need, because this isn't working, and with the Davenport name on the line, and Megan relying on me, failure isn't an option.

I walked to the fridge and stared inside. I'd already had soda last night, and for the most part, I avoided it, since drinking too much tended to leave me gassed during practice and games.

Apple juice and water were the options I had, and I needed more than H2O.

Great, now I'm referring to it as H2O, the way Lyla always does. I smiled as I poured myself a glass of juice, remembering when she and I had been doing one of our first labs, and she'd turned to me and said, "I'm sure you heard about the two guys who tried to order water at the bar."

I'd assured her I had no idea what she was talking about, and then she'd bit her lip, looking like she'd changed her mind about telling me the story. But once I nudged her and said, "You can't leave me in suspense like that," she pushed her safety goggles up her nose, carefully filled a beaker with hydrogen peroxide, and said, "Two men walked into a bar. The first one said, 'I'll have some H2O.' The second guy said, 'I'll have some H2O, too.' The second guy died. Obviously." Her gaze flicked to me. "You know. 'Cause..." She lifted the hydrogen peroxide, clearly afraid I hadn't gotten it.

"Because drinking hydrogen peroxide—H2O2—would be bad," I'd said, so she knew I understood.

She beamed at me. "Right!" Then her smile faltered and she shook her head. "I know it's lame. I just..." She shrugged. "Couldn't help myself. Got the potassium permanganate?"

I handed it over with a cheesy remark about double

bonds, and things went from carefully cautious and reserved to joking and chatting as we worked our way through the experiments. Science wasn't the only thing she made corny jokes about, either. Once she found out I played hockey, she started making puck jokes. She'd greet me with a, "Hey! What the puck's going on?" Or "How did we manage to puck up that experiment?"

I was starting to pick it up, too, often using the P-bomb when we were arguing about movies. If I ever slipped and swore that way in front of the guys, I'd never hear the end of it.

One thing was clear, though, I wouldn't have enjoyed that class nearly as much without her. Guess I should see how much she knew about economics. If she could tell a bunch of micro and macro jokes and help me understand what the hell they even meant, maybe I wouldn't want to stab my eyes out every time I studied it.

Of course, if Lyla was going to keep wearing skimpy outfits, I might need to stab my eyes out to keep from thinking inappropriate thoughts about my sweet, brainiac friend.

Chapter Eleven

Lyla

There he is.

He'd been in the same spot nearly every time I'd come into the library over the past several weeks, always deep in study. And since I didn't so much as know his name, he still totally counted as someone I didn't know. Beautiful Stranger had dark curly hair that got more out of control every time he combed his fingers through it—judging from its current state, he'd been studying a while. Then there were the Buddy Holly glasses that added to the cute nerd vibe. I decided it also made us a perfect match.

My heart rate hitched up several notches as I neared him. *He looks busy studying. I probably shouldn't interrupt.*

But not saying anything was the wimpy way out, and I wasn't taking that way anymore. I smoothed a hand down my tight teal top with black lace down the middle. It slimmed, yet emphasized the fact that I had curves. Unlike last night, I was only showing a hint of cleavage instead of a generous portion. I fought the urge to tug at my jeans. After wearing loose skirts for so long, they felt crazy tight, and the material was so thick. I'll admit they made a better shield than my skirts when it came to cold air cutting through the fabric and leaving my legs covered in goose bumps, though.

All right, I can do this. Ask questions. Deflect the conversation back to him. Sound ditzy. The feminist side of me wanted to argue with Beck that sounding ditzy wasn't necessary, but that was also probably the side of me that never got asked out. I wasn't going to hide the fact that I was smart, maybe just keep it on the DL until we'd had a conversation or two.

"Excuse me? Do you mind if I sit next to you? This spot has the best view of..." I glanced out the window. "The... gravel roof."

Crap. I was already failing. My feet readied to bolt and my palms grew uncontrollably itchy. Then he glanced up at me and smiled. Oh my goodness, his smile was everything I'd dreamed it'd be and more. "Gravel roof?"

Be bold, be bold, be bold. "Okay, that was a lie. I've spent so much time studying that I'm starting to feel like I've been in solitary confinement. Don't worry, though, I'll be quiet. I just feel like breathing the same air."

What the puck? Breathing the same air? Might as well have just said I'm going to dig through your trash later.

His forehead scrunched up, but there was a hint of amusement flickering through his eyes, so instead of fleeing, I forced myself not only into a chair, but the one right next to him. "I'm Lyla."

"Sebastian."

I'd never met anyone named Sebastian. *The Little Mermaid* comment that popped into my head almost slipped out. Clenching my jaw held it in, where it belonged. See, totally getting the hang of this. "So, what are you studying?"

"Calculus."

"I'm a chemistry major, but today I have to devote myself to Emerson and Thoreau." I held up my book as if he'd need proof. After my awkward start, he probably did.

"Well, I'm happy to share my gravel-roof view." He flashed that dazzling smile one more time. "I better get back to studying, though."

"Yeah, me, too." I read through my assignment, only slightly—okay, very—distracted by Sebastian's presence. No wonder I'd avoided group study sessions before. Sure, I had the occasional group project, but never with anyone I'd daydreamed about. He'd become this perfect guy who I'd someday meet and discover that we were, in fact, perfect for each other. Only I never actually thought we'd meet. After resisting the urge to pull up my hair for thirty minutes, I couldn't take it anymore. I finally piled it into a bun on the top of my head, secured it with one of my many pens, and then got busy jotting down notes on everything I'd read.

When I went to cross my legs, I accidentally kicked Sebastian's shin. "Sorry."

"It's okay," he said, sliding his notebook closer to him and erasing whatever he'd written down. I opened my mouth to make a remark about how Einstein was constantly trying to climb my leg while I studied, so I knew what it was like to not be able to stick out my legs, but then I remembered talk of my cat should be delayed if possible.

Poor Einstein. I feel bad acting like he doesn't exist.

I glanced at my watch after another forty-five minutes of silence. If I wanted to get to the hockey game on time, I probably needed to pack it up. That meant this was my last chance to leave an impression. Maybe give him my number.

My tongue felt like it'd been stuck to the roof of my mouth with peanut butter, so I pulled out my bottle of H2O and took a drink. "So, Sebastian, I was thinking…" I leaned in to do the hand-on-the-arm thing, and he turned, and I tried to avoid the collision, but it was too late.

"Ouch!" Sebastian jerked back, rubbing at the long blue pen mark by the side of his eye. I slid the pen out of my hair as if that'd undo the damage.

"I'm so, so sorry!"

"It's okay," Sebastian said, still rubbing the spot. Now what was I supposed to do? Ask him if he wanted to keep that eye? In this instance, more questions probably wasn't the way to go.

"I gotta…" Sebastian started to gather his books.

"I'm leaving, actually," I said, jumping up. "You don't have to move."

Wariness filled every groove of his face, and clearly that magical we-discover-we're-perfect-for-each-other day-dream had become more of a this-girl's-a-psycho nightmare for him.

I shoved my notebook into my bag and rushed out of the library, my nerves still bouncing across my skin, making it feel too tight. *Setbacks aren't unusual when it comes to experiments—every good chemist knows that. Gotta power through and try again.*

And trample some other poor unsuspecting guy.

With a sigh, I pushed out of the library. Looked like I could use some more tips from Beck, followed by a practice session or ten with Whitney.

Or maybe I should just quit before I stabbed someone's eye out.

• • •

Ice is cold. It's something I knew, being very into science and, you know, as a person over the age of three. But I wasn't expecting the seats of the hockey arena to be quite so chilly.

This is what I get for ditching my scarves. Now I freeze everywhere I go. My outfit was much cuter without the coat, but I was too chilly to entirely ditch it, so I decided to go with unzipped, which at least kept it from puffing up around me. Getting a cold and having a runny nose and hacking cough wouldn't help me out right now. Especially since I managed to screw up everything *without* those fabulous side effects.

Most everyone in the rest of the crowd was in groups or couples, so I felt a little odd sitting alone, but luckily I was used to that feeling. And who knew? Maybe afterward Beck could introduce me to his teammates. If one of them had lost a tooth or two, he might even be in my league. A nice perv, as Beck put it.

I laughed to myself, furthering the look of Crazy Loner Girl.

Music pumped through the speakers, and the team skated onto the ice. *So which one is Beck?* Finally I saw a jersey with DAVENPORT at the top—he was number seven. The helmet made it hard enough to make out his features that I wasn't sure I would've been able to tell it was him without the helpful labeling.

I stood, wondering how much of a nerd I'd be if I shouted his name and waved. With the commotion, he probably wouldn't hear it or see me. After crashing and burning with Sebastian, I'd had a moment where I thought I should just skip the game, change into my pajamas, and watch a movie while pounding back raw cookie dough. Despite being solo, I was happy I'd sucked it up, put on an extra coat of mascara and lip gloss, and driven down here. Because with the energy in the air, the zing of skates against the ice, and experiencing firsthand what Beck had always talked about so excitedly, it didn't feel like I was alone.

He was everywhere I looked, and that made me feel like he was next to me, which always had a way of making the stress in my life disappear. His blue eyes flashed into my mind, the intense way he'd looked at me last night, and the warmth that flooded me took the edge off the cold.

I bit my lip and told myself friends could make you feel warmth like that. When my brain immediately argued it was a different kind of heat, I picked up my soda and sipped half of it down, hoping the bubbles and sugar rush would keep me from examining that line of thought too closely.

Chapter Twelve

I tried to play it cool and not look for Lyla—if she didn't come, it was fine. It's not like I needed her here to cheer me on. Even back in high school, my parents only made it to a few games. There were always other events going on at the same time, or business trips to prepare for instead. Megan had dragged her friends to almost every one, though, and when it came to trash talking, my little sister had a gift. She also had one of those whistles that took out people's eardrums. My teammates used to laugh about how they'd never expected so much noise to come from such a little girl.

I smiled at that, thinking Megan would've been pissed if she knew they called her a little girl, especially since she'd had crushes on half the team.

"What was last night about?" Jeff asked me as we slowed our pace—we wanted to be warm, not exhausted. "Why'd you tell me to hit on your girlfriend?"

"My girlfriend?" I frowned. "That'd be some messed up shit."

His eyebrows arched, as if to say, *You're telling me, dude.*

Another loud song started, making me have to shout to be heard over the noise.

"She's just a friend. It was her first big college party, and she was nervous. I thought having you talk to her would make her feel better."

"She was hanging all over you. I thought you guys were doing some weird... I don't know. Role-playing thing to spice up your night or some shit."

Spice up our night? As if I'd need role-playing to keep a girl interested. "She was drunk and wearing heels. She was trying not to fall over, and I was making sure she didn't." I fought back another flash of being on the dance floor, when I'd used the excuse of not letting her fall to pull her against me. I gripped my hockey stick harder, focusing on it so I wouldn't let my thoughts run away with me. "Like I said, we're just friends."

"Well, she's definitely hot," Jeff yelled. The coach eyed us, and we skated back toward the center of the ice. "So it won't be weird if I ask her out?"

I clenched my teeth, breathing through my nose to stifle the irritation the suggestion brought on. "Not weird. But she's my friend, so don't bother if you're gonna be an ass to her." Since I now felt the urge to hit something, I took a practice swing. Without the puck flying through the air, it wasn't as satisfying as I'd hoped. As I looped around the goal, I replayed the part of last night when I'd carried Lyla to my bedroom. She'd been saying the most random things.

Ooh, you have a cool alarm clock.

Wow, I bet these are, like, super-high-thread-count sheets. They feel like silk on my legs. Which had made me think about her bare legs and how soft her skin had felt when I'd brushed it picking her up.

And then, right as I was drifting off to sleep, she'd leaned over the bed, only her outline visible in the dark. *Tell me the truth. Are you secretly a superhero? Because you're muscly and Mister All American Guy, but then sometimes you get real quiet, and I get the feeling you've got a whole secret life no one knows about.*

Without the superhero part, she was more right than she knew. Instead of worrying she'd read me too well, though, I took it for what it was. She was wasted.

"Bring it in," Coach yelled, and when I got to the bench, I spotted Lyla in the crowd.

She grinned and waved. Her fiery red hair hung in loose waves around her shoulders, her makeup was much simpler than it'd been last night, and she had on jeans and her coat. My heart still beat quicker than it should, and a hint of the desire I'd experienced last night rose to the surface, growing stronger the longer I looked at her. The thought of Jeff dating her made jealousy gnaw at my insides, but I couldn't even think about taking her out myself. No one could be a bigger ass than me when it came to dating.

It reminded me of all the reasons I needed to keep myself in check, regardless of revealing tops, hip bumping, and sexy legs.

I shouldn't even be thinking about anything but the game right now. I definitely shouldn't be trying to see which shirt Lyla's wearing under her jacket, or wondering how to find a good excuse to wrap my arms around her again.

In fact, the more I thought about the dangerous line I was walking, the more I thought that maybe I should call up one of my regular hookups and get some space from Lyla.

• • •

My teammates barreled into me, slapping my back and whooping and hollering. With that last score, we'd won the game.

In moments like this, I knew I didn't want to major in business and go on to run D&T. I wanted to play hockey forever. But I also knew that wasn't in my future, and thinking about it would only mess with my head. I had the right here and now, and that was why I intended to soak it in and enjoy it while I could.

I hated that thoughts like that always took the edge off the buzz of winning.

Excitement and the sense of accomplishment that came along with a victory hung thick in the air of the locker room. I planned on distancing myself from Lyla a bit, but she'd come to the game, so I couldn't not go say hi. I was trying to keep the friendship, not piss her off or hurt her feelings.

When I made my way over to where I'd seen her sitting, Jeff was already talking to her. *Wow. He certainly didn't waste any time.*

She smiled at whatever he said, I heard her say something about being "super drunk," and then she put her hand on his arm and leaned in, biting her lip the way she'd done with me—er, practiced on me.

Using the moves I'd taught her. On Jeff. I ground my

teeth. *Lucky prick.*

"No, you were cute," Jeff said.

I set my hockey stick down harder than necessary to break up the love-fest, and Lyla turned, flashing me a dimpled smile.

"Hey, Mister Hotshot Scorer Guy! That was awesome. If I knew that's what your hockey games were like, I would've come to every one of them."

Her enthusiasm soothed my irritation and made happiness rise up to take its place. The on-the-fly nickname only strengthened it. Nothing was normal with Lyla—she practically spoke her own language. I thought of her there in the stands, cheering for me every game, greeting me like this each time, and a pang of longing went through me. Too bad I was acting like a chick, getting all needy and attached.

"Thanks, Ly." *Time to cut the first string.* "By the way, I meant to tell you earlier, but I'm going to have to cancel movie night tomorrow. With all of your stuff this week, I got behind on everything else."

God, the way her face dropped killed me. I could've just said I'd gotten behind. Why'd I have to add in the jab about her stuff? *I'm a dick.*

Further proof that this was the right move, though.

She fiddled with the zipper of her coat, her eyes carefully avoiding me now. "Of course. Sorry, I've totally been monopolizing your time. I'm sure your string of women are ready to come after me with pitchforks."

The words "It's not like that" were on the tip of my tongue, but I swallowed them back, the taste bitter in my throat. At least she knew better than to think of me as a relationship option—that'd be my saving grace with her.

"You know, I'm free for a movie tomorrow night," Jeff said. "If you're interested."

Lyla glanced at him, then me, as if she were waiting for me to say whether or not she should go.

Hell no! Movie nights are our thing! "You two have fun. Just be warned, Jeff, she'll force you to watch movies about sparkly vampires if you're not careful."

"I've got sisters, so I'm unfazeable that way." Jeff nudged her with his elbow.

The smile I had to pull out of my ass probably looked as fake as it felt. "Well, I've got one, and I was still unprepared."

Lyla's head whipped toward me. "You have a sister?"

I stared at her for a moment, wondering how I'd let that slip—I'd been so focused on how much it annoyed me to watch Jeff flirt with her. Not that Megan was some big secret, but first it'd be talking about my sister, and then that would lead to the confession my parents had died, and it'd only start an avalanche of crap I didn't want to go into. I couldn't exactly ignore her question without more questions now, though. "Yeah. She's sixteen." I hiked the strap of my duffel bag higher on my shoulder. "I need to hit the road. Come on, I'll walk you to your car."

I started toward the east exit, but Lyla stayed next to Jeff. "Um, I'm the other way."

"Me, too," Jeff said. He put his hand on Lyla's back. "I'll walk you out."

The blood pumping through my veins turned toxic. I was totally losing it. Lyla held up a finger to him, stepped down the bleachers to me, and looped her arms around my neck. "I just wanted to say good job on the game again," she said. "Thanks for inviting me and taking care of the ticket."

Unable to help myself, I wrapped an arm around her to hug her back, sliding it under the coat instead of over like I should, noticing that my fingers fit perfectly on the curve of her hip. The desire from earlier grew exponentially with her body against mine, a searing trail chasing away the exhaustion from the game. Calling another girl for a meaningless hookup no longer appealed to me—I didn't want usual. I wanted smart and funny, big hazel eyes, and sexy curves.

You can never go there, Davenport, so stop thinking about it.

"And…well," Lyla continued, "I know you already wasted a ton of time on my list this week, but I appreciate it."

My heart tugged, wanting me to take back what I'd said, while my brain shouted to keep up the wall—to put space between us ASAP.

Shit, shit, shit. I'm seconds from ruining everything.

"No worries," I said. "I had fun, too. I've just got homework to catch up on."

"I do owe you, so if you need help, you know where to find me." She started to pull back, then leaned in again and whispered, "How long till Jeff stops being a stranger? Do you think I have to kiss him tonight to cross off number three?"

My hand stilled on her back, and I curled my other one into a fist. "You don't have to kiss anyone you don't want to, Lyla. Why don't you forget the list?"

She frowned, that damned stubborn determination set in her features. "No way. I already made a fool of myself earlier today, but I pushed through and decided to try again instead of letting it stop me, and it actually *worked*. Do you know how long it's been since someone asked me out?"

She shot Jeff a grin over her shoulder and then lowered her voice and said, "I think I'm just going to kiss him tonight."

Everything in me screamed to tell her not to. Jealousy reared its head again, and it had big jagged teeth that it wanted to sink into Jeff. But Lyla was on her road to self-discovery, or self-wreckage, or whatever the hell it was, and I wasn't her boyfriend.

I didn't want to be her boyfriend.

Anyway, I *shouldn't* want to be her boyfriend.

If there was one thing I knew for sure, it was relationships end in disaster, and I wasn't screwing up someone as sweet as Lyla. I'd warned Jeff to treat her right, and while looking at him right now made me want to punch him, he'd be a decent guy for her to kiss.

I exhaled, careful to keep my voice level as I attempted to muzzle the jealousy. "I think he still counts as a stranger. After you force him to watch chick flicks, he's for sure an acquaintance."

A slow smile curved her lips, and it shot me right through the chest. "Thanks, Beck. But just so you know, you're not getting out of those last two *Twilight* movies."

She gave me an attack hug and then bounded over to Jeff.

And all I could do was stand there, hating Jeff a little more by the second and being pissed at myself for canceling this week's movie night so she couldn't follow through on her *Twilight* threat for another eight long days.

Chapter Thirteen

Lyla

"So, you and Beck have been friends for a while, then?" Jeff asked as we exited the hockey arena.

"Yeah, I met him in a class at the beginning of the year, and it didn't take long for us to become friends." Which was why I knew something was off tonight. Or maybe he was always like that after games. Amped up from victory and the thrill of playing or whatever. Except it was more like he was antsy... Maybe the excess adrenaline pumping through his veins made it hard for him to focus or stand around talking.

The first time he'd slammed a guy from the other team into the glass—right in front of where I was sitting—I'd jumped. Beck was already a big guy, and with those hockey pads on, he'd seemed larger than life. If I'd seen that competitive glint enter his blue eyes when he'd stood across from me, I would've run—or skated, as it were—in the opposite direction. He'd thrown other large dudes around like they were ragdolls, and scored three points overall, including the winning goal.

While I'd always considered myself more of a peaceful and can't-we-all-just-get-along person, I had to admit there was something hot about watching guys so hopped up on testosterone fighting over a puck and slamming into each other.

I was really trying to think of it as guys and not Beck. I'd done so well all day, through our greasy breakfast served by a guy who must've been a huge fan of pancakes or maybe a fanatical hockey fan, because he'd given Beck an enthusiastic thumbs-up for just being there. Then I'd gone and put myself out there at the library, not even a second thought to Beck besides his flirting advice. Alcohol-induced lust—that was where last night's fleeting attraction had come from. And the nonstop thinking about his eyes…well, they were what people talked about when they said piercing blue eyes. I'd have to be blind not to notice them.

But watching him play hockey and then the hug after the game, his fingers splayed across my hip… There'd been completely sober butterflies breaking free and flapping their wings. Even now they stirred, somersaulting in my stomach and rising up to flit around my heart.

"Is that about how most of the games go? Back and forth so fast like that?" I asked Jeff, forcing myself to be in the moment so I didn't screw it up with a guy I might actually have a chance with. "Or was that team extra rough?"

"Nah, that's pretty typical. They actually did a better job than most keeping Beck from scoring, but as you saw, he still snuck in a few."

"Hmmm." That was all I had, since I was now thinking of how Beck had glanced at me here and there when he was catching his breath on the bench. He was far too into Serious Sports Mode to give me the full smile, but the crooked half one had still affected me plenty. Despite my best efforts, a crush was developing.

It's all right to have crush-like feelings, as long as I don't act on them.

And what better way to prevent that than to find a new guy to focus on? Luckily, I just so happened to be walking next to another cute hockey player. While on the shorter side, and not over-the-top hot like Beck, Jeff was definitely more accessible as far as I was concerned, as well as a good "beautiful stranger" contender. Plus, he was low risk. I wouldn't be forced to see him later if things went south.

My mind started going over Beck's conversation tips. We'd already discussed Jeff's hobby. Guess that left school. "What are you—"

"Do you—" he started at the same time, then grinned, revealing nice straight teeth. No gaps from a couple being knocked out, so bonus points. His dark hair was shaved nearly down to the scalp, and his eyes were a chocolate brown—pretty much the opposite of Beck.

Who I was absolutely going to stop thinking about.

"Uh, this is me," I said as we reached my beat up, used-to-be-blue Chevy. Driving it required a lot of praying and swearing, but I was happy to have it, especially on chilly nights like this, where walking meant the possibility of losing toes.

I shivered and zipped up my coat the last few inches—it was too cold to think about not covering up my shape. Even though I knew my hair was down, I did a quick check for pointy objects—call it post-traumatic-eye-stabbing stress disorder. If it'd given me issues, I could only imagine how fast Sebastian would run from me the next time our paths crossed.

Jeff put his hand on my car, right by my arm, and leaned in. "You want to go to the movies? Or just rent one?"

"Whatever," I *so* eloquently said.

He pulled out his phone and asked for my number. After he put it and my address into his contacts, he told me he'd pick me up at seven. He straightened like he was getting ready to leave, and I started thinking he might not count as a stranger tomorrow, so I just went for it.

My enthusiasm got the best of me, turning my attempt at number three into more of a mild headbutt than a kiss. I'd gotten the right side of his mouth instead of the center, too, and all I could do was close my eyes and hope when I opened them, I'd either be alone or wake up to find it'd only been a bad dream.

Twice in one day. I should be quarantined.

"Lyla?"

"Sorry." I cracked my eyes open. "If you've changed your mind about the movies, then I—"

Jeff's lips slanted over mine. He pressed me into the car and shoved his tongue into my mouth. It was a little more… wetness than I expected. Once I started participating, keeping my lips tighter to slow the tempo, the kiss turned into something better, and might've even morphed into some feel-up action if I wasn't wearing such a puffy coat.

"See you tomorrow." Jeff gave me one more quick kiss and then he rushed across the parking lot to a black Jetta, and I climbed into my car, grinning like a loon.

I did it! I kissed a guy I didn't know. I'd even initiated it, but considering how disastrously that part had gone, maybe I shouldn't be so proud.

As I drove away, though, I couldn't help thinking that pride-over-checking-off-a-list-item probably shouldn't be the top emotion I felt after kissing a perfectly cute hockey player.

• • •

You know what you get when you decide to be bold and kiss a guy you barely know?

Attacked with his tongue, pretty much the first moment you enter his apartment. Jeff had hardly said a word to me, just dived right in. His tongue frequently traveled too far south, too, more chin-licking than kissing. After several minutes, my skin felt…*sticky.*

"I'm thirsty," I finally said, pushing myself up from the horizontal position on the couch Jeff had eased me into. The urge to squeegee off my chin and lips was strong, but I didn't want to offend him.

I totally take back those times I wished Miles would kiss me with a little more passion. Maybe French kissing wasn't for me. All I knew was I didn't want to do it anymore—not with Jeff, in any case.

But the movie was only thirty or so minutes in, and I didn't know how to leave without hurting his feelings. The television screen lit up one half of his face and I found my-self focusing on the flickering colors changing on that side as I pondered excuses, none of which sounded good enough to use.

"What do you want to drink?" Jeff asked. "I don't have any beer, but I could maybe get a case—my roommate's twenty-one."

"Some simple H2O would be good."

The lines in his forehead deepened as he scrunched it up. "Water?"

Beck always teased me for not just saying water. I should probably work on cutting back my nerdy chemistry references as part of my makeover. Jeff must've figured it out on his own, because he headed toward the kitchen and opened a cupboard.

I quickly readjusted my shirt, cursing its low-cut front. I took my phone out of my pocket, wanting so badly to text Beck. Something nice and melodramatic like *SAVE ME!!!!!!* But he'd already dealt with my crazy list items and attempt at becoming a whole new me all week, and while he claimed he was behind in his classes, I wouldn't be surprised if he had a non-study buddy with him right now.

Plus, I didn't need Beck to save me. I could save myself.

I hoped.

Jeff sat next to me and handed me a glass of water. The second his hand was free, he wrapped it around my thigh.

"Don't you love this part?" I scooted forward, putting my forearms on my knees, trying to curl myself up as tight as I could. I'd never even seen the movie, and, as my shitty luck would have it, that was the moment the lead actor started undressing his love interest.

So now Jeff thought I loved the sex scene. He leaned in and kissed my neck. The woman onscreen moaned and made a whole lot of noise about what was happening.

It was hard to remember a time I'd ever been more uncomfortable—with a pinch of curiosity thrown in. Were there really women who sounded like that when they had sex? Who enjoyed it so much they couldn't get enough? There had to be.

What was I doing wrong?

Not that I'd find out any time soon, because I *so* wasn't going there with Jeff. After the movie *finally* ended, I let Jeff kiss me for a few more minutes, because he was a nice guy, and I was a big wimp who was not as in control of my life as I'd thought.

Come on, Lyla. Be bold. That's the whole point of what you're doing.

I pulled back, lifting my hands between us for an extra barrier. "Uh, thanks for the movie, but I've got a test tomorrow, so I better go." It'd be so much easier to escape if I would've driven myself instead of letting him pick me up. You know what they say about hindsight being twenty-twenty.

Within a few minutes, we were back at my apartment. Before Jeff could lean in for another sloppy kiss, I bolted out of the Jetta and escaped into the safety of my apartment. When I locked the door and sagged against it, Whitney looked up from her spot on the couch.

"You okay?"

I wiped at my chin—seriously, why did it feel sticky? Ugh. "You ever make out with a guy who was a super bad kisser?"

Whitney made a sour face. "Yes. Don't ever let it go further. If they can't kiss, they're awful in bed. Trust me on that."

I sat next to her, kicked off my shoes, and tucked my legs under me. "He *licked* my chin."

"Ew!" She laughed, and despite how badly my date had gone, I couldn't help joining in. Ever since the night she'd helped me with my makeup we'd been spending more time together, even if it was just an hour here and there watching TV or cooking a meal together. "Definitely kick that guy to the curb. You want someone who makes you crave the next time you can kiss him." She leaned back and sighed. "Like Matt. The sex is *amazing*. Better than anyone I've ever been with. Totally mind-blowing, you know what I mean?"

Mind-blowing. Nope. I didn't know. But when she looked at me, I made a noncommittal head wobble she took for a nod.

"I chickened out on bringing up the relationship, though," Whitney said, the defeat heavy in her voice.

Good to know I wasn't the only one who chickened out. "It's okay. You'll know when the time's right, and from what I saw, he's crazy about you."

Whitney smiled. "Thanks, Lyla. I needed to hear that. I've dated so many jerks over the years that I always doubt my judgment. But it feels different this time."

I took a moment to enjoy kicking up my feet, but then everything I needed to get done came tapping on my shoulder, and that made relaxing next to impossible. My bucket list took up a lot of time, and already, my study hours had taken a hit. "Well, I better go and do the studying and homework thing for a bit."

I picked up my shoes and headed into my bedroom. Einstein bounded over to me, and when I dropped my shoes in the closet, he took that as his cue to attack them. I laughed when one flipped over and he leaped backward like it was a snake that'd try to bite him.

"You're such a cute kitty," I cooed as I settled into the chair in front of my desk. I snapped a picture with my phone and almost sent it to Beck before I remembered I was trying to give him a break from my weirdness. Even more depressing, I couldn't think of anyone else to send it to. My parents, I supposed, but then Mom would want to call and talk, and ever since I'd started wearing more revealing outfits, I felt like she'd somehow sense what I was up to and lecture me on how what I wore sent a message to people. I had no doubt she'd think I was sending the wrong one.

Hell, maybe I was, but there was something freeing about it, even if it also made me feel self-conscious at times—I was still working on being okay with putting more of myself out there.

I tossed my phone aside and turned to the piles of books and notebooks on my desk. Literature currently needed the most attention, but instead of picking up my book, I opened my laptop and pulled up my list.

1. New edgier look

2. Do a keg stand (Remember to not wear a skirt that night)

3. Make out with a beautiful stranger (Exact level of making out TBD as the kissing happens)

4. Sing karaoke

5. Dance on a bar (Learn to sexy dance, so I don't make a fool of myself when the bar dancing happens.)

6. Get a tattoo

I'd done three of the six in one week, which I thought was pretty adventurous of me, despite the few missteps and the fact that the making out was less pleasant than I'd hoped for. But between the sex scene in the movie and what Whitney said, I wanted to add one more thing. Seven happened to be my lucky number, too, so it seemed like fate. I also knew this one would probably take longer than a week or two to achieve, so the sooner I put it down, the more likely I'd accomplish it by finals. It'd require both being bold and pushing my fears aside—it'd pretty much be the ultimate way to fully embrace the whole college experience and leave the old Lyla behind.

Do I really want to type it in here? My computer was password protected, and putting goals where you could constantly see them helped you achieve them—it was a proven fact. So I went ahead and typed it, and it definitely looked bold sitting there on the page, the cursor blinking behind it.

7. Have mind-blowing sex

Chapter Fourteen

BECK

This week had been damn long already, and it was only Thursday. Traveling for games on a weekday nearly always messed with the rest of my schedule, but at least we'd killed Dartmouth in the game on Tuesday, and I'd managed to chat with Megan for a few minutes afterward. Apparently she'd had to put up quite a fight against being grounded to be allowed to go. Lucky for both of us, Aunt Tessa had caved when she'd claimed the game as our only family time. Or more likely, she'd caved because she knew she'd never hear the end of it.

I'd spent the last few days playing catch up, with little contact with the outside world besides classes and hockey practice. I'd nearly asked Jeff about Lyla all week, but I didn't want to know. Not to mention it would've come across weird as shit.

What was even weirder, though, was that I'd met a sexy volleyball player at the campus cafeteria on Monday, and I still hadn't texted her, despite her number sitting in my phone, just waiting to be used.

Lyla and I hadn't talked since last Saturday night's game, and each passing day that went by without hearing from her left me more and more on edge. Sundays were our set-aside nights, but we usually sent texts back and forth all week, and the lack of smiley faces and cat pictures from her ate at me, despite the fact that I'd been the one to purposely put space between us.

I'm just worried about her. Gotta make sure Jeff doesn't hurt her. And that her new better-and-bolder goals don't get too out of control.

That's what I told myself when I texted her, anyway.

Me: *How's the party animal?*

I stared at the display for a moment, about to put it in my pocket when it chimed.

Lyla: *Studying like a mofo, but I need a break. Come over?*

I could just imagine the way she'd say mofo—as un-gangster as possible, the words coming out with a dimpled smile.

Me: *Your cat will give me hives. You come over.*

Lyla: *But Einstein LOVES you. Breathing's over-rated, didn't you hear?*

I was about to text "Fine," but then my phone chimed again.

Lyla: *Be there in fifteen or so :-)*

Me: *:{)*

Lyla: *WTP is that?*

Me, now grinning like an idiot: *Me with my sexy mustache, smiling at your smiley face.*

Lyla: *Mustache???*

Me, making sure to outdo her punctuation by one: *Hurry!!!!*

Lyla: *Keep your pants on, dude ;)*

I laughed, all the suckiness of the week melting away. It wasn't like my life was tragic, but I realized how much having Lyla in it broke up the monotony and kept away the sad memories that liked to emerge when it was too quiet. I wasn't going to screw it up by not talking to her, and I wasn't going to screw it up by crossing lines. With her dating Jeff, it'd be like when she was dating Miles—I'd go back to thinking of her as a non-option, and we could go back to our easy hangouts.

• • •

When I opened the door, Lyla held up a bag from Tasty Burger, my favorite burger place in the city. Must've been why it'd taken her so long. "Full disclosure, this is a bribe. If you take it, you're committing to help me check off one of my list items."

"Which one?" I asked, reaching for the bag.

She swung it away from me as she stepped inside the apartment. "I'm not saying until you decide if you're taking the bribe." She removed her coat, revealing a fuzzy purple sweater that hung off one shoulder and jeans so tight I could see the curve of her hips and nice ass. She unrolled the bag and tossed a fry in her mouth. "*Mmm.* It's sooo good."

"You know I could just tackle you and take it."

She took a step back, her eyes going wide, and a predatory urge to do exactly that went through me. If it involved wrapping my arms around her and having her body pinned under mine for a few minutes, even better.

A few long strides and I was right in front of her, my steadily increasing pulse humming under my skin. She was such a little thing, really, and I towered over her. Instead of being intimidated, the way she should be, she set her chin and tucked the bag behind her back.

"Just promise. I drove all the way to *Fenway* for you." Her chest rose and fell, her muscles tensing like she was preparing to dodge if she needed to.

Much longer toying with her, regardless of how fun it is, and I'm going to need to give myself the Don't Screw It Up speech again. "Fine. I promise. Now gimme."

A triumphant grin split her lips. She spread the food out on my coffee table and sat on the couch, a burger in hand. I already knew I'd regret agreeing to whatever it was, but

I'd do it anyway, so I might as well have a burger first. She got me a double, too—I could kiss her. Metaphorically, of course.

She licked ketchup off her lip.

Maybe not so metaphorically. Time to redirect my thoughts. "So, did you get making out checked off the list?"

She wrinkled her nose. "Yeah."

I lowered my half-eaten burger. "You sound about as enthusiastic as if I'd asked if you've recently been tortured."

She huffed out a breath and then twisted to face me. "Look, I'm sure Jeff's a nice guy, but kissing him…well, it was kind of torture. He *licked my chin*, Beck. I'm traumatized for life."

I burst out laughing, and she shoved me. "It's not funny," she said, but now she was laughing, too. "Please don't tell him I said that. He's texted a few times and I haven't answered. I'm afraid I'll agree to see him again, and I can't—I just can't. This is what I get for making the guy think all I cared about was kissing."

Her sweater slipped farther down her shoulder, revealing a hint of a lacy black bra, and suddenly all my blood moved south. She licked at the ketchup and mayo mess that was about to drip from her burger and then took a giant bite that most girls wouldn't attempt.

It really shouldn't turn me on. Curiosity and want sparked and took control of my thoughts.

"Anyway," she said, shaking her hair off her face and reaching for a napkin. "I did check it off, at least. I'm now on the karaoke portion of the list."

"Karaoke." The word was as effective as a cold shower.

"You already ate the food, so you're coming. Tomorrow

night. I checked your hockey schedule, too, so don't pretend you have a game."

"I'll go with you and listen to you sing, but—"

"Ah! Wrong. You're singing, too. That's what the double patty's for."

There were so many arguments on the tip of my tongue, but then she reached out and ran her fingers across my jaw. "It's really more of a scruffy beard than a mustache."

The sensation of her fingertips on my skin made my heart skip a couple beats, and the desire returned. Leaning into her touch slightly instead of moving away felt like playing with fire, but I found myself wanting to see how close I could get to the flame without getting burned.

"I'm glad," she continued, and maybe my imagination was getting carried away, but I swore her voice sounded breathier than usual. "Mustaches always look so pervy." Her fingers strayed from my jawline, tracing the skin right above my top lip, and I forgot how to breathe.

The corners of her mouth lifted. "Of course, according to you, that's just guys letting their true selves show."

I locked eyes with her. Time to let reality creep back in—for both of us. "That's right. You might as well know what you're getting into if you're still set on this quest to hit on guys. We're the worst," I said, making sure to lump myself in with the rest of them.

She dropped her hand and I immediately missed her touch. *I've just gone without too long,* I told myself, the same excuse I'd tried to convince myself of for over a week. But surely getting back out there would at least help take the edge off. *Later tonight I'm definitely texting…whatever her name is.*

Good thing I'd put it in my phone, because I couldn't even picture the volleyball player with Lyla sitting next to me, her knee resting against my thigh. My fingers itched to brush across her exposed collarbone and trace the bra strap peeking out of her sweater. I couldn't help wondering how she'd react. If she'd gasp. If she'd tip her head up so I'd have access to those lips…

Okay. Pulling back before I do something stupid. Way, way back.

"Luckily, karaoke requires more making a fool of myself than hitting on guys," Lyla said, jerking me back into the conversation I forgot we were in the middle of. "Something I'm a natural at." She took a drink of her soda, leaving peach lipstick on the straw and making it hard to keep my thoughts from returning to her lips.

The ice rattled in my cup as I lifted it to my mouth. A cold drink—that'd help.

"I think I'm going to take a mini break from adventures in flirting," she said. "At least until after I figure out how to sexy dance on a bar."

I nearly choked on my soda and had to force the fizzy liquid down my too-tight throat.

If I survived her college bucket list, it was going to be a fucking miracle.

Chapter Fifteen

LYLA

I'd chosen a karaoke bar a ways from campus, hoping it'd prevent running into anyone I knew. A girl about my age was onstage, belting out a Kelly Clarkson song. When no one booed during her totally off-key, laughing-through-the-lyrics rendition, my muscles relaxed a fraction. All the same, I reached for Beck's hand, needing something to hold on to.

He looked down at me, the colored overhead lights reflecting blue, yellow, and red across his skin at intervals. His face was even scruffier than it'd been yesterday, and I wanted to run my fingers across his jaw again. Feel the coarse hair against my palm. Have his breath skate across my wrist as his blue eyes pinned me in place.

My skin heated at the memory, the warmth traveling up my arm and spreading through my entire body, the same way it did yesterday. On top of the residual sensation, he curled his fingers over mine, the tight grip giving me the sense of security I needed right now.

The list must be working because I'd definitely gotten bolder, if only by a fraction. A couple of weeks ago, I would've never run my fingers over Beck's whiskers or grabbed his hand, even if I thought I might pass out without it. Both times I found myself doing it before thinking and talking myself out of it.

Of course, being bold with Beck wasn't exactly my goal—it was good training, though, being able to touch a guy without overthinking everything. Nothing more. Really it just meant I was on track, and knowing how awesome it could be with a friend made achieving my list that much more vital.

That was my story and I was sticking to it.

On the drive over, Beck had joked that he was going to add "Not singing karaoke" to his bucket list. It'd made me laugh, but as I stared at the stage and the people crowded around tables, I was thinking maybe it was the better option.

Beck squeezed my hand. "You realize you can take a few months to finish your list, right? You don't have to do it all in a matter of weeks."

I shook my head. "I'm already a semester behind as it is." Plus, there was number seven to consider. I'd need items one through six to amp me up and gain enough courage to accomplish my most recent addition.

"Always the overachiever." He was teasing, but it dug at the part of me that had to do this. I couldn't explain the overwhelming sense of urgency that'd gripped me since deciding to make the list. If I stopped, I knew I'd never get enough momentum going again to finish. I needed to prove I could be the bold, crazy college girl before I went home and everyone tried to shove me back into the box they wanted to put me in.

Nice. Sweet. Adorable. Smart. Plain.

Talk about a yawn-fest—I almost fell asleep thinking about it.

"No going back." Keeping my grip on Beck's hand, I tugged him toward the front of the room. "Let's sign up before I lose my nerve."

Every time I picked a track from the binder of music, Beck declared it a chick song and told me to just sing it myself. Finally, I crossed my arms and stared at him. "Did you, or did you not, eat that *double* burger yesterday? With fries?"

He heaved a dramatic sigh. "Fine. I don't know most of these songs, though." He flipped the page and something about the smile he gave me made my skin prickle. "Here we go. Flo Rida 'Right Round.'"

"You're rapping? Wow. That's ambitious."

The smug smile curving his lips faded. "Like you're really going to sing a song about a stripper."

I lifted my chin. "Why not? Maybe I'll even act out the motions. Do you think it'll count as dancing on a bar, even if it's more a stage than a bar? Maybe there's a pole around here, too."

His right eyebrow shot up, the shocked look on his face turning me into the smug one—I liked this side of things. "You're not serious," he said.

I took a step closer. "Try me."

A competitive glint hit his eye. "I'm going to put it down on the singing list. And I'm dragging you onstage when they call our names."

A flush of adrenaline curled its way through my body. "Oh, I'll beat you onstage. You'll be the one holding back."

Beck scribbled our name on the karaoke list, along with the code for the song. Apparently, we were singing and rapping about strippers. Bold, to say the least.

Now I wished I'd ordered those striptease workout videos I'd found online. Not that I planned on actually acting out the lyrics—my current goal was to not totally choke at the singing. But maybe they would've given me a few mild dance moves I could use to spice up the performance and distract from the times I couldn't quite hit the right note.

Beck put his hand on my back as we headed to an open table, five fingerprints of heat burning into my skin, even through the fabric of my shirt. "You want a drink?" he asked when a waitress came by.

"Yeah. Something with lots of vodka," I joked.

Without missing a beat, he ordered me an appletini and a beer for himself, along with hot wings and onion rings. Once the waitress was gone, I leaned in and asked, "Weren't you scared she'd card us?"

"I've got a fake ID if I need it. Most of the time if you're confident, they don't bother."

I'd love to think I could pull it off, but there was no way. This was why Beck was the perfect person to learn confidence from. If only I could stop thinking about how much the scruff worked for him, how lately our banter felt more… charged than usual, and how every time he put his hand on my back, I wanted to lean closer and feel more of his body against mine.

Addictive shivers of electricity skittered across my skin and gathered low in my stomach. If I entertained thoughts of pressing into him much longer I might lose my mind and try it out.

Well, if there was one thing I was good at, it was taking that option away by bringing up cats. "Okay, you're going to mock me, but I have to show you this picture. I was looking up bucket list items, and I've even started a Pinterest board for it—"

"You're right. I'm gonna mock you, nerd."

I elbowed him in the ribs. "Hey. That's not even the part I'm talking about." I pulled up the photo I'd saved on my phone and showed it to him.

Beck looked at the cat standing on two legs, its mouth wide open, a microphone photoshopped into its paws. The corners of his mouth twitched like he was trying not to smile.

I poked his cheek. "Come on, a cat singing karaoke is crazy cute. You can admit it. I won't tell."

"I just want to know if he's singing the Kesha or the Flo Rida part." The skin around his eyes crinkled in this adorable way as he finally gave in to the smile. I liked how his whiskers were lighter, a hint of strawberry hue to them— he'd probably hate me pointing it out, though. Not to mention it'd be a dead giveaway that I couldn't stop staring at him.

But the thing was, he was looking right back at me, an indescribable expression on his face that made me think maybe the cat pictures weren't as much of a deterrent as I thought.

I must be tripping. There's no way Beck *is looking at me like that.* Despite my common sense shouting for me to abandon my current line of thinking, longing still wound itself through my body, shaking every one of my senses awake.

Beck draped his arm on the chair behind me, his fingers brushing my neck along the way and his knee resting against my thigh. He placed his other arm on the table, closing off my view of anything but him and bringing his chest against my shoulder. Each sharp beat of my heart attacked my rib-cage, an intoxicating mix of pleasure and pain.

"Lyla," he said, his voice deliciously low, and my throat went dry.

Then his phone rang, popping the cozy bubble that'd formed around us. It almost seemed as if he had to shake himself awake — probably because I had to, and my tempo-rary insanity reflected that onto him. He glanced at the dis-play. "Sorry. Give me a sec."

When he answered, it was with the same tone he'd used when he'd gotten a call while I was in the dressing room. A cold lump formed in my gut as I wondered if he'd ditch me again.

"I've already explained all the reasons why you can't live with me," he said into the phone. "I love you, but we'd drive each other crazy, and you'd only get into trouble. Not to mention the fact that you're mid-semester in high school. And before you ask, you *do* have to graduate, so don't even go there."

Whoa. This just got more awkward than my love of cats and goofy pictures involving them. I suppose the girl could be eighteen, so…at least not illegal? Did she know about all of Beck's other girls, though?

"If you'd just be nice to Tessa, she'd be much easier to live with." Beck glanced at me. He put his hand on my shoul-der, twisted the phone up so the mouthpiece was in the air, and whispered, "Sorry. My sister's determined to win an award for best dramatic actress in a perfectly nice life."

Sister. Relief flooded me. "It's okay," I whispered back. Of course watching him talk to his sister, smiling or shaking his head at whatever she said, only made the crush I was trying to pretend I didn't have grow.

How many times did I have to tell myself that he was the worst possible guy to crush on? I needed his friendship more than I needed to kiss him. My gaze moved to his lips.

I was fairly certain.

He licked his lips.

Damn, I was slipping. Good thing he never would, or we could really screw this up.

"Beck and Lyla are up next!" the emcee announced. "If you guys can make your way to the stage…"

My eyes flew wide as I looked at Beck. No way was I singing that song by myself. *I* couldn't rap. I didn't even know if I could pull off the Kesha part.

"Megan, I gotta go. I'm singing karaoke."

Even with the noise in the place, I could hear her shocked reaction.

"It's not like that," Beck said to whatever had come after her exclamation. Not hard to figure that out. It wasn't like that with us—a good reality check, really. One I obviously needed. The guy onstage waiting for us to come up and take the microphones was a little *too* real, though. The ground seemed unsteady under my feet as I stood.

Beck scooted out right behind me. He held out his hand as if he knew I needed it. I gripped it like a lifeline all the way to the stage, only letting go to take one of the offered microphones.

The music started, and I wished my appletini had arrived

so I could've at least had some of it buzzing through my system. Considering the completely sobering effect the sea of anticipation-filled faces brought on, it probably wouldn't have helped. Beck's part was up first. He cast me a quick *holy-crap* glance before lifting his mic and singing into it.

I echoed his first line, the way my prompter said to, and then we were off and running. The faster the lyrics got, the more Beck struggled. He didn't quit, though, just put a little swagger into it, his confidence and the rapping coming from his lips totally at odds.

I laughed so hard at his performance I nearly missed my cue. Beck moved closer to me and whispered, "Where's the dancing?"

I swiped at him, but he dodged my hit and leaned in again. "You can use me as the pole if you want."

Heat flooded my cheeks—as if I wasn't embarrassed enough. But then I decided what the hell. So I danced a circle around Beck, and the second time he sang, "From the top of the pole, I watch her go down," I slid against him.

He faltered and motioned for me to help, and I obliged, because, well, it was my fault we were up there in the first place. As far as the actual singing went, "complete disaster" fit perfectly. But between the laughing, dancing, and being out of breath, those three or so minutes were some of the most fun minutes of my life.

The crowd clapped and whistled like it was the best thing they'd seen all night—which was nice of them—and Beck took my hand. He lifted it, and then we bowed in unison.

I handed the microphone to the guy running the karaoke, and he called the next name. Our drinks had already arrived at our table, and I wasted no time tipping back mine.

Beck took a swig of his beer and then flashed me a grin that added to the light-headed, overloaded-circuits sensation that'd overtaken my body. "You'd make a hell of a stripper. Gotta work on the taking clothes off part, though."

"Yeah, and who knew you could drop the beats like that?"

The wattage on his grin kicked up a couple of notches, reaching a too-perfect-to-look-directly-at-without-swooning level. "I do try to keep it on the down low. When you're good at everything, it brings out the haters."

"I'd imagine." I bumped my shoulder into his. "Thanks for doing that with me. So far, that's been more fun than the keg stand and making out with a stranger combined." I leaned back in the seat and took another sip of my neon green drink.

"I know I resisted at first, but that was fun." Beck shot me a sidelong glance. "You're something else, Lyla."

"I think the word you're looking for is crazy. Or maybe Queen of Awkward."

His eyes locked onto mine. "Nope. Definitely not the word I'm looking for."

Was it my imagination, or was his face moving toward mine? The earlier attraction, longing, and electricity rose to the surface, mixing with the adrenaline from singing. Dizziness set in and I hoped the world never righted itself again. *Don't think. Just go with it.*

The sound of plates being dropped on the table made me jump. "Need anything else?" the waitress asked.

Yeah, I could've used another minute or two to see where that was going.

But now the moment was gone.

I wasn't even sure it was there in the first place.

Chapter Sixteen

That was close.

The singing, the laughing, the dancing—*holy shit, the dancing.* I'd nearly dropped the microphone when she'd slid her body down mine. Then she'd popped up and given me an evil vixen smile that made me grateful the lights were so dim.

When I'd told Megan I was about to sing karaoke, she'd snarked, "You must really want to sleep with her."

I'd assured her she was wrong, but now I needed someone to assure me. If the waitress hadn't come when she did, I would've crossed over the friends' line and into bad idea territory. While I tried to convince myself the interruption had come at the perfect time, part of me—a big part of me—thought I would've rather kissed her and had to apologize if necessary than wonder.

I downed half my beer in one gulp and reached for the food. Nothing like onion breath to make you second guess if kissing was a good idea. Of course, I did have Altoids for situations like these.

No way, Davenport. You're not kissing Lyla.

"Man, these wings are hot," she said, blowing out a breath. "My lips are seriously tingling."

I picked up one of the orange pieces of chicken, staring across the room instead of looking at her. She'd made it clear she wasn't interested in me like that—it was another reason why I'd let the friendship develop in the first place. She thought I had a steady string of girls, and I did.

Or I used to. I hadn't so much as kissed a girl since Lyla showed up at my apartment, determined to change her college experience. But at the mall she'd made a point of saying how great it was that we were nonentities to each other, and at the party last weekend she'd reiterated that she didn't care about impressing me.

I bet I could convince her differently if I did kiss her—I'd sure as hell do a better job than Jeff's chin licking.

"So, kinda funny story…" Lyla grabbed one of the celery stalks and dipped it in ranch dressing. "When your sister first called, I totally thought it was one of your many women, only I could tell by the sound of your voice that you cared about her. Then, when you said the thing about her being in high school, I started worrying you were dating some jailbait chick."

"Uh, ew." I reached for my drink. "I can find plenty of college girls, thanks."

"Oh, I know. But there was that beat where I was starting to think I didn't know you at all."

I lowered my glass and looked her in the eye. "Lyla, you're one of the few people who really knows me."

She blinked at me for a moment, and when she bit her lip, I could tell she wanted to ask more.

"Go ahead. What do you want to know?" Unbelievable. One lip bite with eyelash batting thrown in, and I was giving her permission to pry into the part of my life I kept secret.

"Do you have any other siblings?"

"No, thank goodness, because Megan's more than I can handle most of the time."

Lyla propped her elbow on the table and cradled her chin in her hand. "I always wondered what it'd be like to have a brother or sister."

I slid an onion ring through the puddle of ketchup on my plate. "Not all it's cracked up to be."

"Oh, come on. I only heard one side of the conversation, but I could tell you adore her."

Cursing myself for opening up this line of conversation, I finished off my beer. I'd order another, but I had to drive later. Which also meant we'd need to sit here for a bit, listening to more mostly awful singing while Lyla asked who knew how many more questions. "Like I said, Megan's a drama queen, but my parents were gone a lot, so it's always been us against the world. I feel responsible for her, and lately she's been getting into trouble. Some kind of teenage rebellion stage, I guess. It always makes me nervous to answer the phone when it's her, not knowing if it'll be 'Hi,' or 'Come pick me up from jail.'"

It was the most I'd ever said to anyone in Boston about my family, and it was a relief to talk about, although there was a part of me screaming to shut up.

"Jail? Seriously?"

"Shoplifting," I said. "More of a prank than anything—not that my Aunt Tessa and I aren't taking it seriously."

"What about your parents?"

And it always comes to that, doesn't it? I glanced at the woman onstage doing her best Katy Perry impersonation, not wanting to see the pity cross Lyla's face. "They…" I cleared my throat. "They're dead."

Lyla placed her hand on my knee. "Beck, I'm sorry. I shouldn't have pried." The note of apology for asking a simple question got to me. Making her feel bad about it was worse than seeing pity, so I dared a glance at her. "Now I get why you don't talk about them."

"It's not just that… Back in Canterbury, we were the family everyone talked about. Whether it was with respect or bitterness or jealousy. Everywhere I went, people would say, 'Oh, that's Richmond Davenport's son.' When my parents died, people talked about it, asked about it—it was inescapable. I got so sick of people fishing for details, or asking how I felt, or wanting to know what our family was going to do about the company…" I ran a hand through my hair, digging my fingernails into the scalp so I could focus on that instead of the fact that all the air was slowly being wrung out of my lungs. "It was nice to come here where people didn't know anything about it."

I put my hand over hers, needing to hold it there and push its comfort deeper. "That makes me sound horrible. That I never want to ever talk about my parents."

The multicolored lights reflected off her eyes and danced across her skin as she stared up at me. "Not at all. It makes you sound human."

Without giving it a second thought, I leaned in and kissed her cheek. "Thanks."

If she knew every nitty-gritty detail, she might think differently. Mom and Dad were flawed, but they were good people, and of course I'd loved them, even if I hadn't told them nearly enough. Everything I needed to do to honor their memory and take over the company like Dad wanted weighed on me. I didn't want to let him down, even though he wasn't around to see me anymore.

Occasionally I wanted to wallow in how unfair it was that I had to deal with responsibilities I didn't want, especially while still dealing with everything I'd lost. I knew there were people out there struggling to pay their bills. People living with cancer. And I was the rich boy who wanted to cry about having to be part of a company that'd ensure my life was always filled with every item I needed and then some. I hated that about myself.

"Do you want to go?" Lyla asked.

The night started out so amazing, the mood light and fun—well, except for my stray thoughts about Lyla's lips and body, but I'd managed to rein those in. I didn't want to leave it like this, and I needed more time to make sure the alcohol was out of my system. I thought of her onstage, singing and dancing. "No. I want you to sing another song."

Apprehension filled her hazel eyes, and I almost took it back, but then resolve replaced it. She gave me a smile I felt all the way to my bones. "Your wish is my command."

If that were really the case, I wanted to take back the singing request and make a totally inappropriate one about her in my bed, naked and underneath me.

Chapter Seventeen

I walked through Whitney's open bedroom door, stepped over the piles of clothes she had scattered across the floor, and tugged up the neckline of the lacy white tank top she'd lent me. "What do you think? I'm not sure it's a good option."

Whitney glanced at me, only one of her eyes rimmed in black—tonight she looked more alt than sorority. "You know, you've been showing off your boobs a lot more lately, but I'm still blown away at how well you hid them for so long. I'd kill for your cleavage."

I flinched at the reference to how much cleavage I had on display—I kept thinking I'd get used to dressing differently and stop feeling a pinch of shame every time I wore something that showed a little skin, but so far, it still loomed there in the background.

"And the white with the leather cuff and black necklace

gives you a mix of virginal with the naughty," Whitney continued, apparently not noticing my shakier-than-I-wanted-it-to-be confidence. "Trust me, guys will go crazy for it."

For months all I'd wanted was to be looked at instead of looked through, but now I wasn't sure I cared what the guys went crazy for. My jeans were so damn tight that I wished for my skirts, and I even missed my scarves. Maybe I'd used them to hide, but I missed the bright colors. And their warmth.

"I'd kill for your butt," I said, hoping it was okay to comment on something like that. "I wish I had more junk in my trunk. Instead it all landed in my hips."

Whitney laughed. "And I wish I had half as much. I guess we all want what we don't have."

"True," I said, exhaling a quick sigh of relief that we could talk about these things. I'd never had anyone to confide in about my body issues, and it was nice to know that even Whitney—who was so confident and beautiful I was intimidated standing next to her—struggled sometimes, too. "Right now, I'm also wishing I knew how to dance better. I still don't feel ready for Sexy Dancing on a Bar."

"All it takes is a little gyrating and hair flipping. As long as you don't fall off the bar, the men in there won't be paying much attention to the moves."

For about the hundredth time this week, I wondered if coming clean about my college bucket list to Whiney had been a bad idea. I'd come home from karaoke, high off the energy of singing and how much Beck and I had laughed. There was the serious moment in the middle about his parents, and I was glad he'd finally opened up a little—hopefully he didn't regret it. But then we'd gotten back to butchering songs and laughing, and the entire ride home, we sang to the radio, all our cares forgotten.

And even though I totally got that the cheek kiss was just a thanks-buddy-ol'-pal, I'd replayed it as I'd climbed the stairs to my apartment.

When Whitney accused me of looking like I was in a "lust daze," I'd panicked and insisted it was just the list, which led to me showing it to her, complete with number seven. Now she was on a mission to find me a bar to dance on, and a guy to get lucky with.

The edges of my phone dug into my palm as I swiped my thumb across the smooth glass again and again. I'd fought the urge to call Beck all day. There'd be no finding a guy for number seven if Beck went, and I was sure he had plenty of other, more exciting options on a Saturday night. But he was my safety net. I knew he'd be there to catch me if I fell. Even if it was falling off a bar in these wicked spiked heels Whitney had also lent me.

But I also wanted—no, *needed*—to be strong enough to do some of the list items myself. Or, you know, with the help of Whitney and lots of alcohol. After going from a drink once every few months to a couple every few days, I felt a bit like a lush.

That's what college is for, right? Drinking, dancing like an idiot. Falling for your hot guy friend and then getting over it by hooking up with someone else.

My roommate finished off her makeup with another coat of mascara, stuck in large hoop earrings, and tucked her ID and money into her bra. "Let's do this."

My "Yeah!" came out a little weak, but the important thing is, I followed after her anyway.

Bring on number five!

. . .

When I noticed Colin, Matt, and the guy whose name I forgot—although the image of him groping Kristen stayed burned in my mind—I stopped so abruptly that Whitney and Kristen barreled into me. Thanks to the extra-tall shoes, we almost went down like bowling pins, but I managed to snag a nearby stool.

"Uh, Whitney, what are those guys doing here?" I asked.

"Well…" Whitney's apologetic expression didn't change the fact that the guy who'd called me fugly and boring was on his way over, and now I'd never have the courage to dance on the stupid bar and cross off number five. "Don't be mad," she whispered, stepping in front of me. "Matt asked what I was doing tonight, and I couldn't lie to him. I'm trying to start a relationship with him."

Right. Not that she'd tell *him* that. It was so stupid.

Said the girl who's out at a bar with strangers to avoid the guy she likes. But that was different. Beck didn't feel that way about me, and we weren't even close to dating. Colin ran his gaze up and down me, lingering on my neckline, and I fought the urge to flip him off. The surge of angry heat surprised me, but I was glad it'd showed up instead of sorrow or raging insecurity.

I should get Beck to show me how to check someone, the way he does in the hockey rink. It'd be so satisfying to slam Colin into the wall right now.

"Damn, girl," he said. "Why'd you dress like a nun the night I came over?"

I rolled my eyes and pushed past him, over to the bar. There was a guy sitting on a stool, sipping what I'd guess was whiskey. Ordering a drink and having the bartender card me seemed too intimidating, but I had another idea for getting what I wanted.

My feminist values screamed at the thought, but when you think about it, using whatever tools I had at my fingertips to get what I wanted was really a way of being in control, right? I leaned on the bar, keeping my arms in tight, so that my cleavage was fully on display. "Order me a drink?"

The guy glanced up, and a creeper smile spread across his face. Ew. I'd already committed, though, and even more surprising, it worked. After a few minutes of small talk and my feminist side—along with all of my other sides—deciding not to do that ever again, I had a Long Island iced tea in hand. As I made my way over to the table where my roommate and her gang were, my phone rang.

Beck's name flashed across the display.

"Hey," I answered, sure the grin on my face was a giddy, twitterpated grin.

"Hey, I've got to talk to you about tomorrow night."

My heart dropped. He was cancelling movie night again. The outings to cross off list items had been fun, but I missed our low-key nights. "I-I understand. You've been spending all your free time with me, and I'm sure you've got other things to do."

"I'm not cancelling," he said. "I just thought we might do something new. The Bruins have a game, and I was thinking of getting tickets. You want to go with me? See how the pros play?"

My heart climbed back up to where it should be, and

now it was fluttering on top of all the moving around. "Yeah, that sounds awesome. Can you teach me to yell things? I wanna yell things, but I don't want to sound stupid. Like when you were playing, I wanted to be all, 'Smash his face into the glass! Trip him!' But then I thought those probably weren't nice things to scream, and I should be giving more game strategy advice from the stands like the rest of the people."

"I'll teach you the right things to yell," he said, and I could hear the smile in his voice. "But I like the one about smashing faces into glass."

"Good to know. How'd your game go this afternoon, by the way? Smash any faces?" It'd started at four, and I'd meant to look up the score, but was sure if I did, I'd end up calling him to either congratulate or console him.

"Did lots of smashing, scored a few points, only had to sit in the penalty box once, and we won by two, so I'm riding a nice high." That meant smiling happy Beck. Or maybe it'd be closed off Beck like last Saturday's game—not my favorite, and after our karaoke night, it'd sting a bit if I encountered that version again.

"Congrats. I had no doubt you guys would come out on top."

"So, what are you up to tonight?" he asked.

The music picked up tempo, more people packed the bar, and according to Whitney, the dancing got into full swing about an hour from now. Plenty of time to get a nice buzz if I could find a way to do so without flashing my assets. "You know number five on my list?"

"Tattoo?" Beck asked.

I pressed my phone tighter to my ear, plugging the other

so I could hear better. "That's six. I didn't think the karaoke dancing counted for dancing on a bar. So Whitney and I are at this dive off Beacon."

"Oh sure, leave me behind for the bar-dancing quest. I feel slighted."

I laughed. "I've made a fool of myself plenty in front of you. I thought we both could use a break."

"You know I'm always here for you, Lyla. Whatever you need. And now I'm worried. Whitney doesn't strike me as a reliable wingman." His voice was so rumbly and deep that it took me a moment to catch up with what he'd actually said. I think the way he'd said my name must've short-circuited a few brain cells, too. It'd sounded different tonight. More... intimate.

Focus, Lyla. No imagining things that aren't there.

I glanced at my roommate. She was on Matt's lap, and they were kissing—nothing too graphic. They were sorta cute actually, and she looked so happy I couldn't help but be happy for her. Maybe that didn't make her the best wing-woman, but I knew she wouldn't leave me stranded, and better yet, she'd dance with me as promised.

I took a big gulp of my drink now that I was thinking about my plan again. *Wowza, the alcohol's strong with this one.*

I swallowed past the burning sensation and said, "Don't worry, I'll be careful. I'm not getting sloppy drunk tonight. I just need enough liquid courage to dance on the bar and get out of here."

Beck was quiet so long I thought the call had disconnected. Then he said, "Watch your drink at all times. And if you need me, just call, okay?"

"Okay." I thought about adding, *Or you could just come down here now.* But that wasn't being strong and independent, and it would make it harder to meet guys who weren't Beck. Temporary flirty fun, nothing more—those were the terms for the rest of this semester so I could accomplish everything I needed to.

I was smart enough to keep myself out of trouble, and I'd learned the skills I needed to snag the attention of a guy or two.

Keeping myself from being embarrassed?

Well, we'd see about that.

Chapter Eighteen

I'd liked it better when I wasn't spending every minute of my free time worrying about Lyla and her list. The fact that she hadn't taken me with her tonight bothered me more than it should. Maybe she could tell I'd been thinking about her differently and she needed space.

I hope she's not letting her grades slip. We had been going out a lot. She was out even more, apparently. *What the hell? I'm worrying about her grades now?*

But the real Lyla worried about her grades. She had her future mapped out, and it involved graduating with honors. She was more serious about her chemistry major than most seniors were—well, serious as in driven. She did love her cheesy jokes. I thought back to the first week I'd met her, when we were studying and she said, "Don't you know? You can never trust atoms. They make up everything."

I'd laughed at the stupid, super nerdy joke. Then, once I'd seen just how smart she was, and how excited she got over an experiment in lab, I thought that she'd do a better job working at the company I was going to inherit than I ever would.

All those months ago, I'd had no clue our study sessions would eventually turn into this. Whatever this was.

I considered heading to the bar, but that seemed like a total whipped guy move. Or worse, stalker. I pulled up my texts—Daniel had sent out a group message about a party his frat was having. Most of the guys would probably be there celebrating our win. I'd keep my phone on and my alcohol intake low, just in case Lyla called for backup, but I needed to get out.

Before I went and did something stupid I couldn't take back.

• • •

The music was loud, the girls were hot, and the alcohol was flowing. A couple of months ago, I would've been in heaven. Or more than likely, I'd be minutes away from leaving with one of the Jessicas, Ashleys, or Taylors who'd come with the intention of picking up someone. Looking around at the girls here, each one bleeding into the next, I kept thinking they paled in comparison to Lyla. And for some reason, she wanted to be one of them. All because some prick had insulted her instead of taking a few seconds to see how beautiful and amazing she was.

A leggy blonde smiled at me. Maybe now I was being the prick who was judging these girls without giving them a chance. And what did I care if they had a great personality? I wasn't into relationships anyway.

Returning her smile, I approached. "Hi, there. I'm Beck."

"Taylor."

What a surprise. I told myself to stop being an ass and dove into the small talk. She was a sophomore, in Si Beta Something-or-other, and majoring in communication. When I told her I played hockey, she said she *loved* hockey. So I asked her what her favorite team was, and she said, "Well, I'm from Florida."

"Oh, so the Lightning or the Panthers?"

A hint of panic crept into her features. Clearly, she'd exaggerated how much she *loved* hockey. Not that I really cared.

"I guess it's more like I love hockey players, because they're so hot." She leaned against me and ran her hand down my chest, sticking out her lips.

Maybe what I needed to fix my sudden inability to not think about Lyla was a blond girl who loved hockey players. I was considering kissing her when my phone chimed. "'Scuse me for a second."

Her lips stuck out farther, into the duckface range. "Don't be too long."

I dug my phone out of my pocket and took a step away when I saw Lyla's name on the screen.

Lyla: *You'll never guess which song's playing.*

Me: *Well don't leave me in suspense you tease*

Lyla: *You should be here to rap it. Flo Rida says all*

the words and it's sooo pretentious.

I grinned, and then I was thinking about her dancing against me, a sexy blush on her cheeks.

Me: *Are you dancing on the bar?*

Lyla: *No dancing yet. Maybe it's a stupid idea. The girls up there look so desperate.*

Me: *Just do it. You'll regret it if you don't*

I knew it meant guys would be ogling her and trying to ply her with alcohol and dance with her for the rest of the night, but I also knew she'd feel like she failed at one of her goals if she didn't go through with it. Plus, it'd make me a douche if I kept her from meeting guys while I was here chatting up girls. So instead, I'd just be a friend who hated the thought of guys putting their hands on her. The kind of hate that'd fester and grow if I let myself think too long about it, so I lowered my phone, intending to get back to the party. But then it chimed again.

Lyla: *I wish you were here.*

My heart tugged at the words, and for a moment I just stared, memorizing the way they looked. If I were there, I could be cheering her on and standing close enough to provide a safe barrier. *I* could be the one dancing with her afterward, her hips bumping mine as she belted out the wrong words to the song.

Want pulsed through me like a hungry predator that

needed to feed. I curled my fist tight, trying to force it away through sheer strength of will. *She needs support, not another guy feeling her up on the dance floor.*

> Me: *Go make some guys drool before you overthink it. I want photographic proof*

Jealousy burned through my gut as I hit send, but at least I knew I'd made the right decision. If the urge to punch someone didn't remain, I might've marked it as a win.

When I was sure the conversation was over, I turned to find the blonde. She was now leaning against one of the frat boys. Apparently she loved them, too.

I shook my head. Lyla really was the ultimate cock blocker. I spotted a few guys from the team and headed over to say hi. We spent several minutes talking strategy for our final games of the regular season. Without hockey, classes would feel like wading through waist-deep mud, my motivation left behind on the rink. Which was why I'd do whatever it took to extend our season as long as possible, first by crushing the competition at regionals, and then making it to the Frozen Four.

Playing in the college hockey semifinals had always been one of my ultimate goals, and if we made it that far, I'd only have to endure one long month of nothing but studying to keep me occupied. Of course, summer would be even worse. I'd already promised Tessa I'd go through the house and deal with the estate things she couldn't.

Then my meetings with the D&T execs couldn't be pushed off any longer, and I could only imagine how mind numbing they'd be. *I'll do it for Dad, though—that'll help get me through.*

At least I'd get to spend more time with Megan. Hopefully we could do more fun hanging out and less lectures about screwing up her future before it even starts.

My phone vibrated in my pocket, and I pulled it out.

A slightly blurry, purple-tinted picture came up. Lyla and Whitney were dancing on the bar, arms draped around each other. The dimple in Lyla's cheek was out in full force—she looked like she was having fun. Judging from the raised arms and back of heads crowding the bar she and Whitney were dancing on, there were also plenty of entertained men.

Me: *You can def cross off sexy dancing on the bar*

Lyla: *:P Headed home. See you tomorrow.*

I was about to type the required smiley face back when another text came up.

Lyla: *Hey, what's your fave food?*

Me: *Sushi. Why?*

Lyla: *Just curious. You know, I've never had sushi. Not sure I could eat raw fish.*

Me: *Before the game. You, me, raw fish*

Lyla: *I don't know…*

Me: *You'll like it*

Lyla: *Ok. It'll be an adventure, anyway. Night :)*

Lyla, all of two seconds later: *I better get a goodnight smiley face.*

Jeez, woman, give me a minute. Instead of the smiley face, though, I hit the camera button to choose the photo I'd saved earlier. I told myself it was too sappy, but I'd saved it, sure she'd approve. Originally I'd planned on showing it to her tomorrow.

Me: *I'll do you one better. Saw this in my FB feed and thought of you*

I hit send, and off went the message, along with the black and white cat staring in the mirror, a determined look on its whiskered face. Across the picture it said CARL, YOU'RE GOING TO GET OUT THERE AND YOU'RE GOING TO CATCH THAT RED DOT.

I just sent a cat picture to a girl. I've officially lost my Man Card.

Lyla: :-) *!!!!!!!!!!!!!!!!!!!!!!!!!*

I grinned like an idiot all the way to my car. Even worse, when I got inside, I pulled up the picture of her dancing on the bar so I could stare at it one more time.

• • •

It was sorta pathetic how excited I was for the hockey game with Lyla, but as I drove down the familiar streets to pick her up, I let myself enjoy my happy buzz. I couldn't wait to see how she liked sushi and what she thought about NHL-level hockey.

Earlier in the week it'd snowed, but it'd been unusually warm today, and even the piles of snow that rarely melted were mere specks of white. I pulled into the parking lot of Lyla's complex and climbed the stairs to her apartment.

Whitney answered the door and gestured me inside. "She's in her room," she said, then she flopped onto the couch and pulled a book and notebook onto her lap.

Einstein came up to me and rubbed his furry head on my jeans. I'd only met the cat a few times, but I swore he sensed I was allergic and decided that meant he should rub hair all over me. With his long wiry gray and white fur, he was kind of cute—or maybe I'd just been looking at cat pictures too long. Great, now I was developing a fondness for felines.

This is what I get for being friends with a girl. I patted the furball's head despite myself and then moved to Lyla's bedroom. I knocked, and when there was no answer, I pushed inside, Einstein so close I nearly tripped over him. "Lyla?"

When her cat meowed at me like I'd personally offended it, I picked it up. He purred and rubbed against me as I scanned the room. Lyla's closet looked like it'd exploded. Shoes were scattered across the floor, there were a pile of shirts off to the side, and several long, colorful skirts hung on her desk chair. Her laptop was open, and I noticed the list up on the screen.

Of course she typed it up.

1. New edgier look

2. Do a keg stand (Remember to not wear a skirt that night)

~~3. Make out with a beautiful stranger (Exact level of making out TBD as the kissing happens)~~

~~4. Sing karaoke~~

~~5. Dance on a bar (Learn to sexy dance, so I don't make a fool of myself when the bar dancing happens.)~~

6. Get a tattoo

7. Have mind-blowing sex

What the—

"Hey," Lyla said. "I didn't hear you come in. I was just finishing my hair and... Beck?"

I turned around and Einstein dug his claws into my arm, apparently wanting down now. I let him go and took in Lyla standing in the doorway. She had her hair in a side ponytail, several loose strands framing her face. The simple white V-neck showed off her curves and hinted at a lace bra underneath, and she had on one of her long hippie skirts. The pink, peach, and red fabric hugged her hips a few inches below where her shirt cut off, leaving a sexy stripe of skin on display.

And all I could think about was mind-blowing sex, mind-blowing sex, *mind-blowing sex.*

"Is this okay? I need to do laundry, so I was running a bit low on options—hockey game probably means jeans, huh? I should've known. I'll change." She started toward her closet and I caught her arm.

"You look nice," I said, swiping my thumb across the smooth skin that didn't help my stray thoughts. "I've missed the skirts and colors, actually."

A slow smile curved her glossy pink lips and my pulse ratcheted up several notches. Then she glanced over my shoulder. Her smile fell and her face went pale.

I winced. "It was open."

"And you read it?" Her voice came out several octaves higher than usual.

"What? I thought I was consulting on the list." I did my best to sound casual, but inside my thoughts and nerves unraveled quickly, exposing my baser instincts. Working to keep control of myself, I cleared my throat. "I, uh, see you added more."

Pink flared through her cheeks. She slammed the laptop closed, holding it down like if she kept it shut long enough, it'd take away what I'd seen.

"Mind-blowing sex?" I couldn't believe I'd asked, but how could I not? It was like dangling a giant slice of chocolate cake in front of a hungry person on a diet and telling them not to take a bite.

Desire rose up as I traced every inch of her with my eyes, from her pretty face all the way down her killer body, fiery bursts of it pumping through my veins. Yeah, I definitely wanted a taste.

"It's just... I... Since I haven't... It seemed like..." She wrapped the end of her ponytail around a finger, winding faster and faster.

Her distress cut through the overpowering sensations her new list item had triggered, and my brain worked to catch up. *Wait? Is she saying what I think she is?* "So you've never...had *that*?"

Lyla's hand stilled and she swallowed, the gesture looking like it took great effort. "It doesn't have to be so much mind-blowing, but that's everyone's goal, right? I mean, if I could even have an…" She shook her head, her entire face red now. "Never mind. This is way too embarrassing to talk about. Let's just go."

"Are you saying…?" The words *Since I haven't…* and *if I could even have an…* tumbled through my mind. Surely her ex-boyfriend had taken care of her. Or was he one of those selfish jerks who only cared if he got what he wanted? The thought sent anger jumping into the tornado of emotions swirling through me. I should probably let it go, considering how close I'd come to crossing lines without this information, but I found myself asking anyway. "You've had an orgasm before, right?"

For several seconds, dead silence crowded the air between us and her gaze remained glued to the floor. "Miles tried," she said, so quietly I could barely hear her. "I think I'm just… I don't know if I can have one."

"That's crap," I said, pissed she'd blame herself. She deserved better—much, much better. "He just wasn't doing something right."

"We tried a lot of things, and…" She shook her head again, still not looking at me. "Can we not talk about this? I knew I shouldn't have typed it up. So stupid," she muttered under her breath.

I hated that she wouldn't look at me. This was supposed to be a kicked-back night where everything else in our life didn't exist—that was why our Sundays together were so important.

So I tried to focus on why I'd come here. Sushi dinner and then hockey. Not to think of all the ways I could ensure Lyla enjoyed herself, starting with kissing that spot where her neck and shoulder met and working my way down. I jammed my hands into my pockets and let out a long exhale—not that it did much to cool my revved up condition.

"Let's go, then," I said. She finally looked at me, the embarrassment in her features clear. She nodded, told Einstein to be good, and then we headed out of her apartment. As I walked after her, I noticed the strip of skin, equally enticing from the back. The curve of her ass. How sexy her neck was with the hair swept off it.

The urge to touch her overwhelmed me, and finally I gave in, putting my hand on her back as I opened the passenger door for her. I spread my fingers more than necessary, sliding a couple just under the hem of her T-shirt.

She sank her teeth into her bottom lip and my pants were getting tighter by the second.

I had a feeling that for the rest of the night, it was going to be next to impossible to stop thinking about number seven.

Chapter Nineteen

As soon as the hostess sat us in the restaurant, I stole a peek at Beck. He'd hardly said a word since we'd left my apartment.

I'm such an idiot. I never should've put number seven on there.

How was I supposed to know he'd come into my room? Usually he just texted me to say he was in the parking lot. He'd been standing there in his black Henley, letting Einstein rub hair on it, and I'd thought it was possibly the hottest thing I'd ever seen.

Now I could hardly look at him. I wasn't sure why I hadn't immediately shut down the conversation. It was like my mouth thought explaining would make it better, when it ended up doing what it did best instead: made things a hundred times more awkward.

I wanted to hide in a dark hole and never come out, but the only thing I had near me was a menu. Unfortunately it was one of those skinny ones that didn't make a good cover. My heart seized as I caught sight of the prices.

"It's on me," Beck said, and I wondered if I was really so easy to read. "Get whatever you want."

No matter how many times I read the menu, nothing sank in, so I dropped it on the table. "It's all weird with us now. The silence is killing me."

"It's not weird," he said. I raised an eyebrow, and he sighed. "It doesn't have to be weird." He reached out and put his hand over mine. "I'll admit I was a little…shocked. But now I want to enjoy dinner and the hockey game. I'm gonna teach you how to talk trash, remember?"

I nodded, thinking about how warm his hand was and the way it totally enveloped mine, while wishing I could stop the constant thoughts like that. In hindsight, choosing a hot-yet-smart hockey player for a friend might not have been the best choice. I mean, there was only so long I could resist that combo, right? But that just brought me to thinking about how much he meant to me, and how lost I would've been my entire first year of college if I hadn't met him. "Swear it's not going to be weird now."

Did he mean to brush his thumb over my knuckles? My pulse didn't mean to leap over it. "Stop saying the word weird. It's weird," he added in a teasing tone.

I bit back a smile.

"Now, tell me about the dancing," he said, sliding his hand off mine and over to his side of the table. His finger tapped against the shiny wood and I had trouble not focusing on the motion and the way it made the muscle in his forearm jump. "Did you make out with any strangers? Or was that a one-time thing?"

Talking. Normal. I could do this. I forced my gaze up to his face and took a quick fortifying breath. "Whitney and I got up on the bar for a couple of songs. The guys went crazy when we danced together. They kept yelling for us to kiss."

Beck's hand knocked into his water glass, and he barely caught it from spilling.

"We didn't do it," I said. "Jeez, what is it with guys? I'm your friend, and even you're drooling over the idea."

"You're my friend who happens to be pretty and female. You do realize being your friend doesn't mean I don't have a penis?"

I exhaled, deciding it was best not to respond to that—his clear blue eyes, the scruff, and that little indentation in his cheek when he smiled were getting to me plenty without thinking about involving other body parts. So there'd be no fixating on how I could see the hint of definition in his chest even through his shirt, or how firm those muscles felt under my hands the night of the party. How they'd look and feel without the shirt in the way…

Damn it, not *going there, remember?*

I cleared my throat. *Where were we again? Oh, yeah, the other night at the bar.* "As for the making out with strangers, that was a one-time thing. Jeff keeps texting, and I feel bad, but I've been ignoring him—the kissing was just so awful."

"Yeah, he'd probably not be a good choice for number seven either."

I shot him a glare. "Not helping the not-weird thing!" My thoughts about shirtless Beck weren't helping either, but I'd take that to my grave. And now the image of Jeff coming at me with his tongue mixed in, leaving my emotions so confused that they didn't know which way was up anymore.

Is it going to be like this from now on? I don't know if I can take it.

Beck scrubbed a hand over his face, the flustered gesture mirroring the way I felt. Then he leaned back in his chair and crossed his arms. "Come on. Might as well get it out in the open. Then we can move on."

Our waitress chose that moment to show up to take our order. After a brief discussion about types of sushi, and getting a backup teriyaki chicken entrée for me in case I couldn't handle raw fish, Beck and I were alone again. Except for the ghost of our previous conversation hanging over us.

The air was thick with tension and the question of who was going to say something about it first. The longer we stared at each other, the harder it was for me to not squirm in my seat. Finally, I broke. "Look, number seven is… It's just something I want to try, okay? But I'm not going to jump into bed with just anyone to cross it off."

Amidst the dancing on the bar and the attention that it brought, I'd looked around at the sea of unfamiliar faces and realized I didn't want to sleep with some random dude just so I could cross off an item. "I still don't want a serious relationship or anything, but I'd rather wait than force it. I need it to be someone I'm attracted to, whose kiss doesn't gross me out, and I need it to be with someone I trust. Not a total stranger."

I glanced around and then leaned in, keeping my voice low. "Even if the chemistry was off the charts, I know I'd still freeze up if I wasn't comfortable with the guy. And I don't think that would help accomplish my goal."

Beck stared at me as if someone had put him on pause, so completely motionless I swore he'd even stopped breathing. I waited for him to say that wasn't how it worked, or maybe give me advice on how to pick a person for a fling. Instead, he leaned in, mimicking my conspiratorial posture. "I just want to make one thing clear, and then I'll leave you alone about this."

My breath stuck in my lungs, thick and suffocating.

He scooted his chair closer and cupped my cheek, and my lungs gave up working altogether. "Nothing's wrong with you, Lyla. You just haven't been with the right person yet."

My skin was on fire, and an ache traveled down my core.

Then trays of food were slid in front of me, a variety of colors and textures I didn't recognize.

Beck's fingertips dragged across my skin as he slowly lowered his hand, leaving a tingly trail of heat. He gave me a reassuring smile that only deepened my conflicted feelings about him yet somehow calmed me as well, thanked our waitress, and picked up his chopsticks.

He snagged one of the circular pieces with rice and colored sushi inside a green wrap. "Try this one first." He extended it to me, his gaze steady on mine. "Trust me."

• • •

I flinched, grabbing onto Beck's arm as the fight on the ice escalated. I'd stood with him and the rest of the crowd watching the hockey game, but hadn't expected the bombs the players threw at each other. The crowd cheered, egging on the Bruins player, who was landing way more punches than the guy from the Canadiens.

"Aren't the refs gonna stop it?" I yelled over the noise.

"They will when one of them hits the ground," Beck said. My confusion must've showed on my face because he added, "The fights are half the fun."

"Yeah, if you're not the one being punched."

He laughed. "You take some, you give some. It all works out."

The fight wrapped up and the refs sent the players to their respective penalty boxes. As Beck and I settled back into our plastic seats that always squeaked a bit when they went up and down, he shot me a smile. "I thought you wanted to yell about smashing faces. What? Change your mind about liking it rough?"

My cheeks heated, and even Beck flushed once he realized what he'd said. "I mean…" He gave a half laugh, half cough. "Anyway." He pushed his fist to his mouth and shook his head.

I bumped him with my shoulder. "I like the checking and the shoving, but I'm not so sure about the punching. That one player was bleeding."

Beck shrugged like it wasn't a big deal.

I pulled the coat he'd lent me tighter—I'd been a bit distracted by the overabundant awkwardness and embarrassment as we'd left my apartment, and had totally forgotten mine. His was cozy and smelled like him, which was comforting and torturous all at the same time. "Have you left the ice bleeding before?"

"Yeah, it happens once in a while. But I've still got all my teeth." He flashed me an over-the-top grin. "And only a few scars." He rubbed at his eyebrow, and I leaned closer to examine the raised white skin cutting across it. "There are times I can hardly move the next day, but that's part of the fun."

"Fun? And what about fights off the ice? Are those fun, too?"

"I don't get into those if I can help it—I like to get it all out on the ice. But make no mistake, I'd win. Wherever the fight went down." He bumped his shoulder into me, the way I'd done to him, and I couldn't help returning his smile.

Somewhere between starting my crazy bucket list and here, he'd begun to let me in, little by little. I was gradually getting to know the real Beck, and he was even more awesome than the guy I'd known the past several months. Going to his favorite restaurant and having him explain every dish made me feel like I knew him better, too—I liked how excited he got when he told me what raw fish I had to try next, and how proud he was when I gave it a thumbs-up instead of a thumbs-down. Apparently I was more of a beginner level with the "barely sushi" California rolls coming in as my favorite.

Then there was being here with him, watching his face light up during the fast breaks and noticing the way his brow would crinkle when the Bruins lost the puck. He also gripped the armrests whenever things around the goal turned intense. I doubted he'd brought any of his string of girls to an NHL game, but maybe that was just my wishful thinking. Either way, the passion shining in his eyes made it clear how much he loved the sport.

"Is this what you want to do?" I asked. "Play for the NHL?"

The happiness in his expression faded. "It's not in the

cards."

"It's not Vegas. If you want it, you make your own luck."

"It doesn't always work that way."

The raw pain in his voice scraped at me. I didn't understand, and I wished he would explain, although I knew he wouldn't—he was shutting down. Letting the mask descend. Maybe if I really pushed, but the last time I had, he'd told me about his parents. I assumed that had something to do with his statement, and it made me even more curious, but I wanted him to go back to being happy.

So when one of the Bruins players scored, I screamed, "Suck it, Canadiens!" I turned to Beck. "Was that good trash talk?"

Beck draped his arm around my shoulders and curled me close. His scruffy chin brushed my cheek as he said, "Cutest trash talker ever."

A pleasant shiver ran down my spine, and I started wondering if something was happening between us. We were closer than we'd ever been, but I had trouble gauging if that meant we were moving beyond friends. If he felt the pull between us and the same desire to be more.

Hope was so dangerous. It beckoned to me now, whispering to just let go with the guy whose breath was warming my neck. Be bold. Twist my face a couple of inches so that our lips met.

But if I jumped and discovered no safety net waited for me at the bottom, I wasn't sure I'd ever be able to get back up.

Chapter Twenty

BECK

Lyla and I had been missing each other all week. Either I was busy with practice, classes, and games—we had one on both Friday and Saturday this week—or she had study groups or projects due. After spending so much time together the previous few weeks, the days without her seemed especially long and boring. Coach was pushing us extra hard lately, too, so add being able to hardly move to the list that was making everything suck.

All I wanted to do was soak my sore muscles and see Lyla. If she said she was busy, I was going to drive over and tell her it was too bad as I hauled her out of her apartment— that like it or not, I needed her.

Figured I'd go for the subtler, asking nicely method first, though.

Me: *I'm gonna soak in the hot tub before our movie.
Grab your swimsuit and meet me ASAP*

Lyla: *Be right there.*

Me: *Smiley face. LOL. Other required text things*

Lyla: *(_E=MC2_) Do you know what that means?*

I stared at it. Obviously it was Einstein. Energy. *Is she
asking if I have energy? Saying I don't? Saying she doesn't?
Or that she does?*

Me: *Tell me, Einstein*

Lyla: *Smartass*

For a second, I thought she meant I was a smartass for
calling her Einstein. Then I realized she meant the original
text, although she'd probably say it applied to both. I grinned
like an idiot, thinking she couldn't get here fast enough. The
girl was like crack for good moods, and I desperately needed
a fix.

I tugged off my clothes and changed into my swim
trunks. Thanks to being rammed into the goalpost during
last night's game, a large bruise had formed down my left
side. I'd still sent the puck across the line, so that was all that
really mattered.

The complex I lived in had an indoor pool and hot tub,
which was especially nice in the winter. I made my way down
to it, and had only been soaking for about ten minutes when

Lyla showed up. She tossed me a quick "Hey" and started peeling off layers. First her coat, then her T-shirt. The bikini top was brightly colored and gloriously tiny, with a beaded bow in the center that begged to be untied. Good thing the jets covered me from the waist down right now, because *holy shit*. She shimmied out of her pants and I got lightheaded.

This wasn't exactly the relaxing soak I'd planned—not that I was complaining. She wound her hair into a bun—she actually had an elastic band to secure it this time—and stepped down the stairs, hissing when the water hit her skin. "Hot."

Yes, yes you are.

"I was feeling bold when I got this swimsuit—or thinking I wanted to be, anyway—but I'm starting to rethink if it was a good idea." She looked down at her perfect breasts. "I feel like I'm one wrong movement away from a wardrobe malfunction."

She was trying to kill me now, I was sure of it. Surely she couldn't be that oblivious to the fact that I'd had trouble not staring at her lately. Not to mention the way I couldn't keep my hands to myself whenever she was around. Even now, my brain spun for an excuse to touch her.

If she'd noticed, she certainly didn't show it. She sat next to me and started talking about her week and classes, and I tried to follow, but really all I could do was stare, mesmerized by the water clinging to her skin. When I reached over to grab my bottle of Gatorade, Lyla moved closer and put her hand on my side. "What happened?"

Her skin against mine. Her lips so close.

"I..." My breath grew so shallow I didn't think any oxygen was managing to reach my lungs. "Got slammed into the goal post during last night's game. It's why I wanted to come out here and get heat on my muscles."

A crease formed between her eyebrows as she tipped her head and studied it, her fingers lightly brushing down the red and purple bruise. "Looks painful."

I swear, I was about to lose control right there in the hot tub. Capture her lips with mine, press her against the side, and just give in to everything I couldn't stop thinking about. This was a bad idea. Or the best idea ever. Who could think right now anyway? "It's not so bad."

She sat back and I immediately missed her touch. I needed to get this out of my system. Get *her* out of my system.

"I brought my laptop so I can show you the tattoos I've picked when we're back in your apartment. What do you think?" She stood and ran her fingers over her hip, and the overwhelming urge to do the same slammed into me. "Here? Or maybe up my side?" Her fingers trailed up to the tiny string holding her bikini top in place.

My throat went bone dry. "I hear the ribs hurt."

She stuck out her lips and then sat back down. "There's also my back. Not lower back, but more upper back or shoulder. It depends on what I go with. I know people will say that butterflies or flowers are so cliché, but when I look at other things, I think, man, I don't want that on my body forever. So who cares if they're overdone? I want what I want."

I want what I want. I know I shouldn't, but I do. I didn't want to screw up our friendship, but the constant wondering what it'd be like to cross that line had ruined my focus, not only when we were together, but every day. Even hockey didn't shut it out anymore.

Plus I'd told her I'd help her with her list—it was a weak justification and I knew it. I clung onto it anyway.

"Lyla?"

She glanced up.

"Do you trust me?" I asked.

For what seemed like the first time all night, she actually looked at me. I watched her throat work a swallow. "You know I do."

I moved closer and hooked my hand around her hip. "I want to help you out with number seven."

Her hands came up on my arms, and her voice came out as shaky as I felt. "Beck." Her gaze locked onto mine, and she licked her full lips. I could see the hesitation, but as I slid my hand around to her back and splayed my fingers on her bare skin, the rise and fall of her chest grew faster and faster, so I knew she wasn't unaffected. "Could you even—I mean, I know you don't find me attractive that way, and—"

A laugh escaped my lips. "You're kidding, right?" I pulled her tight against me, against my giant hard-on. She gasped, digging her fingernails into my skin, only making me harder. "You've been doing this to me every time we're in the same room, lately. I can't stop thinking about it, and seeing your list…it only made it worse. I want to show you what you've been missing."

"Oh?"

I traced her bottom lip with my thumb. "That's the goal."

Her skin blushed all the way down, from cheeks to neck to chest. Fire spread through my limbs, awakening every thought I'd tried to suppress these past few weeks. I was about to get carried away, but I knew I needed to draw lines before it was too late.

"I'm not a relationship guy. I can't be your boyfriend. If we do this, it's got to be just sex."

She turned her big eyes up to me, and I waited for her to tell me she couldn't. That we shouldn't.

Instead she pressed closer, bumping her hips into mine. "Okay."

Chapter Twenty-One

LYLA

Time ground to a halt as Beck lowered his lips to mine. One hand remained on my back, drawing me closer, as his other cupped my neck. The warmth of his skin soaked into mine. He pressed his thumb to my chin, tipping it up as he parted my lips with his.

Heat wound through my body, short-circuiting my nerve endings and all thoughts besides the here and now along with them. I needed closer. *More.* I looped my arms around his neck, bringing our bodies tighter together, and threw myself into the kiss, matching each stroke of his tongue.

He groaned and turned us so that my butt was against the wall of the hot tub. He moved his lips to my ear and I clung onto him as he whispered, "I think we better move this upstairs."

Beck gripped my hips and boosted me out of the water.

I scrambled for my towel, patting myself dry as quickly as possible. Then I gathered up the rest of my belongings, my heartbeats tripping over each other.

Beck came up behind me, slid his arm around my waist, and kissed the base of my neck. I leaned back against him, fighting all the sounds that wanted to burst from my lips. Luckily no one else was around, but who knew when someone from the complex would decide to go for a swim?

"Come on," Beck said, catching my hand and tugging me toward his apartment. The cool air against my wet skin took away the edge of the haze I'd experienced when Beck kissed me.

Rational thoughts were poking at me, tapping my shoulder and whispering that this might end up going all kinds of wrong. Sex and friendship didn't mix. Beck made it clear he didn't want a relationship, and despite my goal to remain unattached as well, I already liked him way too much. But I've *never* been kissed like that, and my body was still humming. I could only imagine what it'd do if we took things further.

You only live once. Be careful who you pretend to be. No regrets. Fools rush in. Every saying I'd ever read flew through my head, one telling me to go for it, the next warning me to slow down. I still wasn't sure exactly who I wanted to be, or even what style I wanted to commit to. All I knew was that I trusted Beck, and if I didn't go through with this, I'd always wonder. If anyone knew how to deliver mind-blowing sex, I was sure it was him.

So screw everything else.

As soon as the door to his apartment closed behind us, he pushed me against it and kissed me again. The thin fabric of our swimsuits was barely a barrier at all, and I gasped again as I felt his erection against me—the fact that I could even do that to him gave me a surge of confidence. I reached up and undid my bun. My hair brushed my shoulders as I shook it out.

Beck reached around my back and gripped the bow holding my bikini top in place. "If you want to stop, you better tell me now."

I ran my hands across his toned chest, down his abs. Too many lines had already been crossed to simply go back to the way things used to be, and between the kissing and the chemistry that'd been building for weeks pulsing between us, all I could think was *more*. "I don't want to stop."

He yanked the string, undoing the bow there, then made quick work of the one behind my neck. In one fluid motion, my top slid to the floor. I tried not to think about how many perfect bodies he'd seen. Despite trying to become more confident, and the many low-cut tops I'd worn over the past few weeks, I was acutely aware of every flaw I'd wished away before. My pulse hammered so loud in my ears it was all I could hear.

I leaned in for another kiss, figuring at least then I wouldn't be quite as exposed. It had the added benefit of feeling his skin against mine. We headed to his bedroom, a tangle of lips and arms and legs. Beck laid me gently on the bed and peeled off my bikini bottoms. He kicked out of his trunks and then all I could do was stare at his ridiculously in-shape naked body.

Wow.

He leaned over me and kissed his way down my neck, over the swell of my breast. I whimpered when his tongue flicked my nipple. How embarrassing. He moved to kiss the other one, a million amazing sensations going through me when he did the same to it. He slid his hand down my side, over my hip, and then his fingers dipped lower.

I clamped my lips together, fighting the urge to moan.

Suddenly Beck stopped the intoxicating circling of his fingers and I froze, wondering what I'd done wrong. *Oh no, he's changed his mind. And now that he's seen me naked, I'll never be able to look at him again.*

"Lyla?" He lifted himself onto his elbows and his blue, blue eyes bored into me. "You and I are the only people here. The only one who's going to hear you is me, and I want to. It lets me know what you like. If you don't like something say so. Or just tap me on the shoulder. Okay?"

Exposed. I was naked on top of being naked in a whole other way. But it was a relief, too. That he knew me so well. That he'd given me permission to let go, something I should know how to do by myself but had never quite figured out. I nodded, and then Beck slid his hand between my thighs again. I let out a breath, dropped my head back on the pillow, and didn't bother hiding any of the sounds that wanted to escape my mouth.

He slid a finger inside me and then his mouth was over my center, warm and hot and causing pressure to build faster and faster. I gripped the sheets and let everything else go. Thoughts, worries, my inhibitions. I focused on the desire coursing through my veins, on the tingling surges taking over my body. Heat pooled low in my stomach, and every inch of my skin prickled in the most delicious way.

"Yes," I moaned, lost in the sea of sensations I'd never felt before. Then everything came undone inside me, rocketing me over the edge. "Beck, I…" Oblivion took over, every part of me screaming at once, and then I sank deeper into the sheets, a floating puddle of a girl, unable to catch my breath, while thinking I didn't need to breathe anyway.

Beck leaned across me, his bare skin warm and solid against mine. He swept my hair off my face. "You okay?"

"Uh, yeah. That was…" I closed my eyes, my breathing still too erratic to form complete sentences. *That* was what people talked about. Why they'd miss class to have sex. Suddenly it all made sense. I'd never imagined it could be so, so…the words to even describe it escaped me. "*Mmmm*. I'm more okay than I've ever been, like, *ever*."

When I opened my eyes, it was to his drool-worthy grin.

I ran my hands down his ridiculously cut abs, smiling when the muscles twitched under my fingertips. I followed the dark trail of hair and then gripped the shaft of his penis. His eyelids fluttered, and then he made a low growl that sent a spark of excitement through my stomach. He reached into his side table and took out a condom. Once he had it on, he cupped my cheek. "Same rules. You talk to me, and no holding back."

I arched against him. "Less rules. More doing."

A slow smile curved his lips, and then he kissed me as he entered me. As he thrust deeper, I cried out. When the position wasn't quite working and I needed to shift, he propped a pillow under me. I wrapped my legs around him and rolled my hips, finding a rhythm with him. Oh yeah. I'd definitely been doing this wrong before, because it'd never felt like this.

Within a few minutes, I was screaming again, the orgasm completely different than my first, but just as amazing.

"*Lyla*…" The control slipped from Beck's features. His

fingers wrapped around my wrists, digging into my skin as he found his own release. He slowly lowered himself onto me, his weight pressing against me in a way that made me want to wrap my entire body around him and never let go. He kissed the curve of my neck as his breaths gradually returned to normal.

Then he rolled onto his back, arms crossed behind his head, and his eyes drifted closed, giving me the chance to take in every detail about him. From the slight indentation on his chin, to the way his Adam's apple bobbed up and down, to the planes of his torso, and the way lying back like that made the muscles in his arms stand out.

Beck and me in his bed, completely naked and covered in a sheen of sweat. The entire scene almost seemed like a dream. An amazing dream that I hated to end. But I didn't know the rules, and he'd made it clear it was just sex.

The last thing I wanted him to think was that I'd get clingy now. I sat up. "So… D-do you still want to watch the movie, or I can just go home and—"

Beck grabbed my arm and tugged me down next to him. "Not so fast. You've got to enjoy the afterglow."

Testing the waters, I reached out and ran my fingers down his chest, then let my hand rest on his stomach. "I don't know the rules." I couldn't believe I'd said it out loud—I never would've had the guts with anyone else—but this was too important to ruin, and I did better with well-defined boundaries. I *ruled* at following rules.

He covered my hand with his. "No matter what happens, we're friends first. I hope you know how much having you in my life means to me."

Happiness bubbled up in me. I turned so that I could

rest my chin on his chest and look into his handsome face. "Well, you're not much for talk of feelings…"

He shrugged a cute, what-can-you-do shrug.

"But right back at you," I said.

"Good. Now that that's settled…" He pushed me over to lay flat on my back and then rolled onto his side. "I didn't get long enough to worship your naked body." My skin burned every place his gaze touched. "You have the most amazing boobs." He kissed the top of each one, his whiskers lightly brushing my skin and sending a swarm of butterflies through my belly. "I could write a sonnet about them."

"Iambic pentameter and fourteen lines even?"

His eyebrows drew together. "That's what a sonnet is?" he asked, and I nodded. "No, screw that. How about an ode? Are there rules to odes?"

I laughed. "It depends if you're going Greek ode with three stanzas, but I think the term is used more loosely nowadays, if you're looking to go for the lazy version."

"Definitely the lazy one." One side of his mouth kicked up. "Love that you know that, by the way." He cleared his throat. "Ode to Lyla's boobs—wait, I don't want to sound too crass. Let's go with Ode to Lyla's Breasts."

"Much classier," I said with a laugh. My stomach growled and I quickly put my hand over it. "Just ignore that."

"I think that means it's movie and ice cream time." Beck got out of bed, pulled on a pair of boxer briefs and his jeans, and picked up a shirt off the floor. "Don't bother with pants. We're going super casual for movie night tonight."

I stood and stopped him as he started to pull the shirt over his head. "Then don't bother with a shirt."

"Deal." Beck lifted it off and then put it on me. When

we got to the living room, I grabbed the bag I'd brought and pulled on my underwear. Then I headed to the kitchen, where Beck was dishing up ice cream.

I watched the muscles in his back move as he fought with one of the cartons—must've been frozen solid. I bent down and kissed the large bruise running down his side and he shot me a sidelong glance. "Maybe that'll make it better," I said.

Beck handed me a bowl with cookies and cream ice cream and nudged the chocolate sauce toward me. I wondered if that meant no kissing outside of sex time. Friends didn't do that, right? Then again, it wasn't his lips.

Which I was now thinking about gliding down my skin. Time to start making my own boundaries to stay in line with my goal of temporary fun and no expectations, and to keep from getting hurt. I wasn't even sure we would have sex again. But I knew one thing for sure. Getting lucky number seven crossed off the list was something I'd most definitely never forget.

Chapter Twenty-Two

BECK

After weeks of no sex and hardly being able to think straight when I was with Lyla, my mind was finally clear again. Even better, I now got to kick back with my friend and enjoy a movie and ice cream, no pressure. I couldn't remember the last time I'd watched a movie with a chick I'd slept with.

We settled onto the couch and I turned on the newest Fast and Furious movie, waiting for her protest. On cue, she shot me a look. "There're at least as many hot guys as hot girls in it," I offered.

She pressed her lips together, moving them to one side and then the other. "Fine."

I wanted to kiss her, but that seemed too much like a boyfriend move. If this was going to work, I needed to create boundaries. Friend time versus sex time. When she shivered, though, I couldn't help myself. I pulled her legs onto my lap and leaned over them to try to warm her up. And maybe so I could feel her soft skin against my bare chest again.

When I set my bowl down on her thighs, she squealed.

"Cold!"

I tapped the bowl on her other leg before setting it down on my coffee table. As the movie wound down and Lyla shook her head and muttered about how anyone with a basic knowledge of physics would realize the move they'd made jumping from one car to another would be impossible on several levels, I fought the urge to kiss her again—she looked damn sexy in my shirt.

Instead, I turned off the TV and patted her knee. "Didn't you say something about tattoos? You want me to check them out, or do you want to do that another time?"

She glanced at her phone. "It is getting kind of late. Guess we'll save it for next time." She swung her legs off me and got dressed, facing away, suddenly shy—I was going to have to cure her of that. If we ever did this again, that is. She took a pencil out of her bag, wound her hair into a bun and stabbed it through, then handed me my shirt. "Maybe Wednesday after your hockey practice? Then you can help me figure out what to get and where, and we can find a parlor with lots of good reviews."

Yeah, that wouldn't keep me up tonight thinking about every inch of her skin at all.

• • •

Three nights later, Lyla showed up at my door wearing a cream dress with colored stitching that ended mid-thigh. Tall brown boots came up over her knees, leaving only a few inches of skin exposed. It was her old style, but modern at the same time, and without hiding her body. As I took her in, the only thing I could think about was running my hands through her fiery hair and then sliding them up that tiny skirt so that I—

"Hey," she said, charging inside and flopping onto the couch. She opened up her laptop. "So, here are some of the tattoos I picked out. I need your input."

Working to shift gears on where my thoughts were headed and move them to where hers were, I walked over to the couch and sat next to her. A girl on a mission, apparently, she didn't bother looking at me. Just clicked through several pictures of flowers and butterflies in different colors and sizes.

"When I talked to Whitney, she was like what's the point unless people see it? So she votes for something like this…" Lyla pointed to a large floral tattoo with swirls. "But then I was thinking that this isn't for other people, it's for me. Plus, that'd take a long time, and it'd probably hurt like crazy.

"I'm thinking one of the watercolor tattoos instead, because they're really cool. Like maybe this one…" She clicked to a lotus flower. "Or this one." I wasn't sure what kind of flower it was, but it was little and pink and orange.

"I think the second one," I said. "It looks like you."

She glanced at me and grinned. "I think that's my favorite, too." I thought maybe she'd take a beat to say more, maybe greet me properly—which I wouldn't be opposed to including a kiss—but then her attention went right back to the laptop. "Okay, I've been looking up reviews for tattoo parlors and…"

Her words blurred as I stared at the zipper on the inside of her boots. My fingers twitched, wanting to slowly zip it down and see her legs again. For them to be wrapped around me. How could she focus on anything else now that we were finally in the same room again? Ever since Sunday night, I'd hardly been able to stop thinking about the sex and how amazing it'd been.

Suddenly I started worrying it hadn't been mind-blowing for her. Maybe it was just okay, and I was as clueless as her ex. Maybe she couldn't even cross it off her list. *No, she wouldn't have faked it. What would be the point? Not to mention, I'd felt it when I'd been buried deep—*

"Beck? Are you listening to me?"

"Honestly? No. Your dress is short and those boots are hot." I nearly laughed at the way her mouth dropped open. "Like you didn't know how sexy you looked when you put that outfit on."

"Sexy?" she asked, as if she'd never heard the word before.

I nodded and closed the space between us, my attention consumed by her mouth. The instant her soft lips were under mine I groaned in relief. "I've always had a thing for skirts, with their easy access." I slid my hand up her thigh and when she spread her legs, I stroked her with my thumb.

I took in the shaky breath she exhaled and slipped my tongue in to meet hers. Within a couple of seconds she was rolling her hips. Telling me when to go faster or slower. The boots came off and so did the panties, but the skirt stayed on. When I mentioned that I'd always wanted to have sex against the wall with a woman in a skirt, she said, "Well, how convenient. I just so happen to have a skirt on, and there are several walls in here."

I wasted no time backing her up against one. And as one of my sexual fantasies came true, I made a note to figure out what hers were, so that I could make sure I fulfilled every. Single. One.

Chapter Twenty-Three

LYLA

I stood in front of my closet, surveying the contents and trying to mentally put an outfit together. *It's not like I'm his girlfriend, so it doesn't matter what I wear.*

Over the past few weeks, I'd had a *lot* of mind-blowing sex. Once in a while I'd get caught up in thinking about Beck, and admittedly they weren't always just-friends or just-sex-buddies thoughts. Now he'd asked me to go to a party the hockey team was throwing, and anxiety churned through me, along with question after question.

Would he hold my hand?

Kiss me?

Hit on other girls in front of me? *Man, that'd suck.*

Just remember, no matter what happens, he thinks I'm sexy. A calm washed over me. He liked me for me, and he'd never cared much what other people thought. I did know he had a thing for skirts, though, so I pulled on the short lavender lace one I'd bought during my last shopping excursion — I was definitely going to need a summer job to pay off that credit card — along with a white tank top and a dark purple beaded necklace.

As I was deciding yay or nay on a shimmery silver headband, my phone rang. Last minute I decided yay — the headband added bling and volume to my hair, so win-win. I picked up my phone, expecting Beck, but Miles's name was there instead.

"Hello?" I answered, wondering if he'd called by mistake. He'd texted to check in a few times since we'd broken up, but we were both busy, so I hadn't heard from him in months.

"Lyla. Hey."

I moved to the mirror, teased up the hair behind the headband, and then reached for the handmade purple and blue chandelier earrings I'd picked up at a street fair last year. Apparently Miles wasn't going to say more than *hey*. "How are you? How's school?"

Speaking of school, I really need to check my grade for that lit test that totally snuck up on me. Surely I didn't do as badly as it felt like I did.

"School's good," Miles said. "I'm busy, but my grades are good. And I like my professors." NYU had always been Miles's dream, and at one point I'd thought about going there, too. But I'd gotten more scholarships for BC and that pretty much sealed my fate. At first we told ourselves the distance wasn't *that* much and we could find a way to make it work, but that was before we tried to find the time to visit back and forth.

"Cool." I slicked on some lip gloss and then glanced at

the time. Beck should be here any minute.

"I miss you."

My body stilled.

"I know we broke up because of the long-distance thing, but… No one gets me like you, Lyla. No one's as driven or as focused—so many girls here aren't even that serious about college. They just think it's party time."

Driven. Focused. Serious. How many times had he told me he loved that about me? Was that even me anymore? Maybe I was slipping—I had been to lots of parties lately. A tinge of panic pinched my gut. This past month, I hadn't dedicated as much time to my classes as usual. I wasn't flunking, but I wasn't excelling either. This whole bucket list was supposed to prove that I could be serious about college and more relaxed about life at the same time. Only balance had been trickier than ever since Beck and I had entered our friends with benefits arrangement.

And now that I had Beck, I didn't even miss Miles anymore—it'd been weeks since I'd thought about him.

But I don't really have *Beck.* I didn't know what to say, so I went with the polite. "Yeah, I miss you, too."

"You should come visit me," Miles said. "It's only three hours."

"Or you could come visit me." *Wait? Why am I inviting him here? Do I even want to see him? I think it'd just be awkward.*

"My car's in the shop. I think it's dead. Seriously, you'd love it here. You've got to check it out."

My car was limping and hacking up a lung, but not quite dead. "Yeah, maybe."

A knock sounded on the front door. I cut through the

living room and swung it open. Beck had on a vintage blue T-shirt that stretched nicely across his chest and brought out his eyes. He'd shaved today, and while I liked scruffy, shaved was equally nice.

"Looking sexy as usual." Beck's fingers skimmed the hem of my skirt. "Love this."

Oops. I hoped Miles didn't hear that—didn't want to hurt his feelings when he was having a vulnerable I-miss-you moment. I held up a finger to Beck. "Hey, Miles, I've got to go. I'll look at my schedule and call you later. 'Kay?"

"Potassium to you, too," Miles said with a laugh. "Talk to you then."

Yes, I appreciated the periodic table humor as well as the next chemistry nerd, but for some reason it didn't make me laugh this time. I guess we'd used it too much over the years.

I hung up and smiled at Beck, and with him in front of me, his sexy compliment echoing through my head, my earlier anxiety melted away. "I'm so ready to party. The non-drinking version, of course, since I'm the designated driver and all." I hooked my hand in his elbow. "It's your party, so you can drink if you want to."

"Deal." As we headed down the stairs to the parking lot, Beck asked, "You still talk to Miles?"

"I haven't for a long time. He just called out of the blue. Said he wants me to visit."

Beck barked a laugh. "Yeah, right. Like you're going to drive all the way to New York for a booty call when you get nothing out of it."

I wanted to tell him to be nice—and to add that not every guy expected a booty call—but that wasn't what our relationship was about. So while I'd told Whitney last night over pedicures and a cheesy romance movie to stop wondering if she should call Matt her boyfriend and just ask—he'd claimed to be busy more and more and she was in full meltdown mode about it—I realized I was a total hypocrite. I couldn't even talk to my best friend about the guy I was having sex with. Because, silly me, I'd gone and made them the same person.

• • •

No surprise, the party was big and loud. The guys had about a month without games as they trained for regionals at the end of March, and apparently they planned on letting loose during their mini-break. Whenever Beck ran into one of his teammates, they greeted each other with a variety of fist or chest bumps, with the occasional bro hug. He introduced me to everyone, but other than a hand on my back here and there as we wound through the crowd, we didn't touch.

There was no hand holding and no kissing.

Beck and I were circling the crowd when a tall brunette in teeny-tiny shorts shoved a total jock-type guy, sending him stumbling into our path. "You're such an ass!" She loudly accused him of checking out another girl, and he tried to placate her with, "Baby, it's not like that!" Her response was to storm off, and then he chased after her, leaving our pathway clear once again.

Beck shot me a sidelong glance, the *yikes* expression on his face clear. "That's relationships for you. Aren't you glad we don't have to deal with that?"

"Totally," I said, but another couple who stared at each

other like there was nothing else in the world snagged my attention. The guy had his hands in her pockets, so there was definitely some feeling up going on, but when he laughed at whatever she'd said and kissed her cheek, I could tell their affection went beyond the physical.

There was no doubt they were together, and clearly they didn't mind who knew it. Miles had always held my hand, had always introduced me as his girlfriend. I didn't realize how much I missed small gestures like that.

I've got to stop thinking that way. It'll just screw up the good thing Beck and I have. Besides, now I was glorifying my relationship with Miles, when the truth was that we'd had plenty of issues, several of which went back to the fact that sex with him left us both frustrated enough we'd stopped having it very often. He'd been the one to bring up the breakup, too, as if having a girlfriend in another state held him back somehow, which I supposed didn't make it as mutual as I liked to pretend.

"You want another drink?" Beck asked, eyeing my empty soda cup. "I'm going to grab another."

"Sure."

His hand grazed my back before he headed toward the drinks—the contact made my skin hum, and I told myself it was as good as hand holding, even if it didn't necessarily announce we were here together. I watched him maneuver through the crowd and how he smiled and nodded at people as he passed. Not shoving, but always nice. Intimidating enough by size alone for most people to move out of his way.

The sex *was* amazing—there was no denying it. A week ago, he'd asked me what I wanted to try. If I had any fantasies he could help me out with. At first I'd said I didn't have any, and that I liked what we were doing, which was true. But when he'd pushed again the other day, I'd finally blurted out the thing I'd thought of a few days after he'd asked. "I...I want you to wear all of your hockey gear. Then I..." My face had burned and I'd turned away, shaking my head.

Beck had put his fingers under my chin and tipped my face up to his. "Then what, Lyla?"

"Then I want to take it off you, one piece at a time."

I'd waited for him to laugh, or look at me like I was crazy, but he'd simply kissed me and told me to hang tight while he changed into his gear. Stripping it all off and telling him exactly what I wanted had been empowering, and my body trembled with desire just thinking of the sex that'd followed.

But I still wished that once in a while he'd simply hold my hand. Or kiss me when we weren't naked or on our way there.

Longing wrapped around my heart and squeezed. I shouldn't be thinking of what I didn't have. Beck was crazy hot, he made sure the sex was as good for me as it was for him, and I knew if anyone tried to hurt me, he'd tear them apart.

We were friends, and friends first, and that was as important to me as to him. Even the fun conversations and easy hangouts with Beck had faded a bit, though, replaced by a blur of sex. It made me feel less like a friend and more like a girl to pass time with until he got bored—I wasn't delusional enough to believe he wouldn't eventually move on to someone else. I closed my eyes, hating that I felt stupid for not being happier about how great my life was right now. That I wasn't pulling off no-strings-attached, no-expectations-or-getting-serious fun.

Was I still open to another adventure around the corner? Or would I turn it down so that I could continue to fool myself about what was happening between Beck and me?

"Lyla, hey."

I opened my eyes to Jeff. *Shit.* "Hi!" It came out way too high, with the edge of panic I was trying not to show.

"Haven't heard from you in a while."

A hand pressed to my back, the familiar cologne and the way my nerve endings jumped to attention letting me know Beck had stepped up next to me. "She's seeing someone now," he said.

I glanced up at him, my heart fluttering at his words. All that worry for nothing.

"I hardly even get to hang out with her now," Beck added. "She's always with her new boyfriend."

The flutter changed to more of a stutter with a splat. There was an awkward beat where Jeff just nodded, then he took himself and his sticky tongue somewhere else.

"Figured that'd be the easiest way to get him to stop asking you out," Beck said, handing me a cup filled with Coke. "You must've really put some kind of spell on him."

Really? That's *the easiest way? Instead of simply admitting you and I are spending all of our time together?* Suddenly I wondered if I was his dirty little secret. The girl he didn't want to think was sexy. He'd made it sound unbelievable someone could be so wrapped up in me, too. The confidence I'd built up since starting this whole endeavor slowly leaked out of me. I hated that I wasn't stronger, but it didn't stop me from feeling the opposite.

I sipped my drink, wishing it were laced with something more powerful than sugar, even though, logically, I knew alcohol wouldn't solve the mess I'd gotten myself into.

All around us there were people laughing, drinking, and practically humping in corners. There were a lot of beachy bimbo types wearing clothes that made my short skirt and tank top seem like a burka, and most of them were draped over Beck's teammates, sometimes two or three to a guy.

"You know, I'm kind of surprised you'd bring me when you could pick up so many girls here," I said, hating I'd let it come out.

Beck lowered the drink he'd been tipping back and his eyebrows drew together, genuine confusion filling his features. "Why would I need to do that? I have you."

For what? Hookups day and night? Or is there more? Now I was wondering if he was having sex with other girls on the side, on the nights I was busy cramming several subjects into my brain at once. The thought made my stomach lurch.

"Hey, Beck." The words were icy cold, and when I turned to see who the feminine voice belonged to, I recognized the blonde I'd interrupted him with all those weeks ago. He'd introduced us, but I couldn't remember her name. She was giving me the same look she'd given me then, too—like I was dog crap she'd gotten on her shoe. More hatred flickered through her eyes as she turned to Beck. "I'mma big girl. You could've just told me you had a girlfriend. You didn't have to ignore me for a month like I was some desperate clinging idiot."

Judging from the slurring and slight bobble, she'd surpassed the level of alcohol intake that allowed her to keep her inside thoughts from coming out of her mouth a while ago. She was still clinging to the cup in her hand, though.

Her lip curled as her acerbic gaze moved to me. "For her of all people."

I guess I should take comfort in the fact that Beck hadn't hooked up with her in a while, even if that made me the target of her rage.

"Monica, you've had too much to drink," Beck said, keeping his voice low. "This isn't Lyla's fault—she and I are just friends. I was up front about what you and I were doing from the beginning, and you said that was what you wanted, too."

"You're an asshole. All guys are such fucking assholes." She wobbled and Beck reached out a hand to steady her. She jerked away, and whatever was in her cup sloshed over the edge. "Don't come crawling back to me when you get bored with her." With that, she walked away, every few steps sending her drifting farther to the right.

Beck scrubbed a hand over his face. "Sorry. I should've realized she'd turn into one of the clingy ones, regardless of what she claimed."

Instead of trying to come up with a response, I wrapped my arms around my middle, wondering if eventually *I'd* just be one of the clingy ones, too.

"See, there's another reason I came here with you. You're so much cooler than other girls."

Or was I more of a pushover who kept her feelings to herself?

Damn it, why can't I go back to not worrying about this, and just having fun, no labels or pressure? I forced my feelings into a dark corner to be explored later. We were at a party, and it was time I started acting like it. The beat from the music flowed through me, and I bobbed my head to it, bumping against Beck until he grinned. No matter what else was going on, seeing him smile made me feel better.

"Davenport!" Someone yelled across the room. "Get over here."

We headed toward the guy waving him over. Apparently there was a big beer pong tournament going on, and they wanted to recruit Beck. Within a few minutes, teams had been drawn up and Beck was seated across the table from one of his other teammates.

I thought about mingling while he was playing, but thinking of being "on," meeting new people and trying to make small talk exhausted me. And what would I do in the unlikely event of a guy hitting on me? Would Beck care? Either way, I wasn't interested in dealing with it tonight. So I watched as Beck played, getting louder and more flushed with every drink.

"You want next?" One of the hockey players—Daniel, I think—asked me when his and Beck's game wrapped up.

"Oh, I'm driving," I said with a shrug.

Beck grabbed my hand and pulled me onto his lap. "She'll play, and I'll drink for her."

I glanced over my shoulder at him. "You know that I've never played, right?"

"One more college experience to check off your list, then."

"It also means I'll miss a lot. And that you'll have to drink a lot."

"There are worse things that could happen. Now, go on." Beck dropped the Ping-Pong ball in my hand. "Just aim for the middle until you get the hang of it."

Aim. Right. It didn't help that I was distracted by being

on Beck's lap, one of his arms loosely circled around my waist. It wasn't really a boyfriend-girlfriend gesture—and it hadn't happened until he'd gotten a buzz going—but at least I didn't feel like he was embarrassed of me. In fact, I was feeling other things, and I might've rocked back and forth more than I needed to.

Beck had just finished yet another cup, thanks to my poor beer pong skills, when he brushed my hair aside, moved his mouth next to my ear, and whispered, "You're killing me in this skirt. You know that, right?"

Goosebumps swept across my skin. I turned my head to his, our lips so close, and I wondered what he'd do if I kissed him in front of everyone. His hand circled my thigh, and want throbbed through me, making me crave being alone with him.

"My turn," one of the guys yelled, and we were forced out of our seat. Beck pulled me aside, and with the way he was having trouble walking in a straight line, it was clear the drinks were catching up to him.

I'd never seen Beck really drunk before. He was giggly. Handsy. "You might have to carry me to my room tonight, Lyla. Make sure to take advantage of me." He laughed, and I shook my head, laughing, too.

Maybe having the perfect boyfriend who got you and your humor, was happy about a long-term relationship, and gave you so many orgasms you could barely move afterward was a myth. Maybe you had to choose one or the other. A guy who wanted to be your boyfriend but was slightly boring or licked your chin, or the no-attachments guy with the sizzling physical chemistry.

With Beck moving closer, his hand sliding over the

curve of my butt, I'd have a hard time saying which I wanted more—my hormones were screaming too loud to consider the safe boyfriend option.

So maybe I'm learning I'm more of a relationship person than a no-strings sex buddy, but I can hold back my expectations and that longing for more for a little while if it means more time having this.

Besides, the safe choice failed me before. Might as well know the danger before it unexpectedly dumps me on my butt.

"You know why else I wanted to come here with you?" Beck asked.

I looked up into his half-lidded eyes and then went ahead and ran my hand down his cheek the way I wanted to. "Why?"

"This is my last season of hockey, and I wanted to celebrate the end of the regular season right. Our regional matchup is against a tough team with a better record, and honestly, it could be my last game ever."

My heart tugged at the sadness weighing down his words. "Wait? What? Why wouldn't you play hockey next year?"

"Family stuff. I might need to stay in Canterbury. Start learning more of the business." He wound his fingers through my hair. "I'll miss you if that happens. You're the only person I can really talk to. Around you, I get to be just me."

So much of what he was saying confused me, but that last line hit me hard. He was the only person I got to be just me around, too. Whether it was the cat pictures, chemistry jokes, or the hidden side of me that I'd never shared with anyone before—the side that wanted to conquer my fears and be bolder. To embrace my sexuality and experience all the things I had with him. Because of him, really.

So instead of holding back and questioning if it broke the rules of our arrangement, I tipped onto my toes and pressed my lips to his. As he drew me closer and deepened the kiss, I closed my eyes and melted into him until the music, the crowd, and all my worries and cares faded away.

Chapter Twenty-Four

BECK

My heart pounded in time to the loud music, the bass echoing through me as I ran my hands down Lyla's fine ass, pulling her closer and swirling her tongue with mine. She slid one of her legs between mine and I moaned into her mouth. My thoughts went fuzzy as she lightly bit at my bottom lip.

There really was something different about Lyla lately. It wasn't just the hair or the clothes or her goal to be bolder—maybe that's what it'd taken me to finally see her, and I felt like a chump about it. More than that, though, she finally understood the power she possessed, and in turn, power over a guy like me, who'd do pretty much anything she asked right now. She was more confident and hands-on than she'd ever been, and it drove me wild.

I'd been trying to keep the lines to sex or friends, none of this in between stuff, but with her breaths becoming mine, her tongue stroking mine until my body burned with the need to have her, I didn't care anymore.

When we came up for air I glanced around—there'd probably already be other couples hooking up in every room. We could wait for them, but then someone might bang on the door and interrupt us, and I didn't want to be interrupted, or for her to hold back. At this rate, though, I wasn't sure I could make it all the way to my apartment.

Lyla ran her hands up my chest, and her hot breath hit my neck a moment before her lips did. "You wanna get out of here?"

My cock leaped at the suggestion. Then she ran her hand over the bulge in my pants and I nearly came right there. "Feels like you do."

I'd created a monster. A beautiful, sexy monster. All I could do was nod and follow her closely as she started through the crowd, trying not to sway too much and failing.

In the parking lot I went to step over a concrete divider, and the next thing I knew I was eating pavement, my knees and hands stinging.

"Shit, I'm sorry," Lyla said, squatting next to me and putting her hand on my shoulder. "Are you okay? If I had realized you were having that much trouble walking, I would've stuck closer so I could catch you."

"Catch me? I would've crushed you, Lyla."

"But I'm supposed to be taking care of you the way you did me when I was drunk, and, well…" She clamped her lips as she took me in, and then she laughed. She quickly covered her mouth with her hands. "I'm sorry, now that I know you're okay, it's…" She laughed again, her shoulders shaking. "I'm just glad I'm not the only one to make a fool of myself when I'm drunk."

"Fool of myself?" I pushed up to my knees and wiped gravel from my torn up palms. "What are you talking about? I'm suave as shit."

This got another round of giggles, and she laughed so hard that she braced herself against me to keep from tipping over. That made *me* laugh, and then we were two idiots laughing in the middle of a parking lot, our clouded breaths filling the air around us. Wiping tears from her eyes, she straightened and held out a hand. I took it and let her pull me up. Then I wrapped my arm around her shoulders. She put hers around my waist and leaned her head on my shoulder.

"You're perfect in your not perfect," she said, kissing my cheek.

I wasn't sure if it was being drunk that made the words hard to put together, or if she wasn't making sense, but I liked the way she said it anyway.

• • •

"I think you need to come meet with the lawyer over your spring break, Beckett," Aunt Tessa said when I answered the phone. Lately, she'd been on me to do it, and I kept putting it off, telling her I'd take care of it over the summer.

"Why doesn't he just run it by you?" I asked as I continued on my way across campus—I'd spent an hour in the weight room after practice, so my arms and legs felt like jelly. "I don't know enough to make those kinds of decisions."

"He says another lawyer has a client who insists on meeting with you as soon as possible. I asked him what it's about, and he said he doesn't know, but that the woman insists on meeting with you in person, and claims it's a family matter, not business."

That was probably what those calls from Mr. Hawthorne, my dad's lawyer—and I suppose mine—were about. At first I thought Megan had gotten herself into trouble again. Once I'd heard another person's lawyer demanded a meeting, I blew it off. If this was my last semester at BC I wanted to be living in the moment, not have one foot in the business, doing a half-assed job at both things.

I pushed into the library, and the woman at the front desk glared at me and pointed at the cell phone. "I gotta go. I'll come down next week. Will you set the meeting up for me? Just nothing too early in the morning."

"I think that's the right choice," Aunt Tessa said, the relief in her voice clear. These days, almost every sentence she said to me started with "I think," followed by a long list of everything I needed to take care of, and it was all apparently urgent. I appreciated her holding back till now at least. I could tell the stress of making decisions in a company she had no desire to be part of was wearing on her. I wanted to say, "Welcome to my world," but it wasn't her responsibility, it was mine. Without her helping out with Megan, I'd have to say good-bye to even more of my independence, so the least I could do was take care of whatever this was.

"Young man." The librarian had followed me. "*No* cell phones."

Aunt Tessa had already disconnected the call anyway. I showed the woman that I was putting it in my pocket and made my way to the second floor. I scanned the desks until I found the messy bun held up by a pencil. Lyla had recently dyed it again—something about roots showing—so it was extra bright. She had on the chunky brown frames she wore when she'd been studying for so many days in a row that her eyes couldn't deal with contacts anymore.

I came up behind her, ran my hands down her arms, and kissed her cheek. "I thought I'd find you here." Ever since she'd scored a low B on her literature test, she'd freaked out and started logging in crazy long study hours—the other night I'd had to pry the book out of her hand and drag her into the bedroom to get her mind off classes for a while.

"It feels like I live here lately." She tipped her head back to give me access to her neck, and I took advantage, kissing her soft skin. Since the party a few weeks ago, things had been more like this. What I imagined most relationships were like, but with us, there was no pressure or questions like, "Why didn't you call me?" or "Where are you?" with our lives revolving around each other. And we still hadn't spent an entire night together, although I'll admit I'd been tempted to ask her to stay a couple of times, not wanting to let go of having her next to me all night. Which was the exact reason it was important to keep my mouth shut about it.

"So come over," I said. "I'll even order pizza with your completely unnecessary, nasty warmed-up tomatoes on top."

"Mmm. That sounds amazing. But I have to meet this guy at my place in an hour."

My muscles tensed, even as I told myself to be cool. "A study buddy?"

"No, a friend who's got a friend who does tattoos, so he said he can get me a deal. We're going to check out the shop and then I'll probably make an appointment."

Jealousy spiked through me, and all those possessive-relationship-type questions I thought we were above ran through my head. *Where'd you meet this douche? Why didn't you call me? Am I supposed to buy this "just a friend" shit?*

"Why do you have your serious hockey face on?" Lyla asked, spinning in her chair to face me, one leg tucked up against the back.

I shook away the thoughts trying to turn me into a crazy person and looked down at her. "I don't. I knew you'd decided on the tattoo and getting it on your hip, but I didn't realize you'd picked out a place."

She grabbed my hand and laced her fingers through mine, which helped the stinging heat pumping through my veins cool a bit. "I haven't. I was just talking to Jason about his tattoos when I saw him in the cafeteria today—he's got them all up his arms and on his chest and ribs…"

The toxic heat returned. How'd she know about the tattoos on his chest and ribs? I'd always thought I was above this jealousy shit, but all I could think of now was Lyla with some tatted-up dude. The envy I'd felt before we hooked up was nothing compared to the punch that hit me now. I wanted to tell her she couldn't go, which I knew she didn't deserve—she could go anywhere with anyone she wanted. The caveman side of me didn't care right now, though.

"…going to text you to see if you wanted to go with us, but then I got caught up in studying and forgot about it."

Forgot. I didn't like that she could just forget to text me either. I didn't know what the hell was going on with me, but it blew. I wanted to claim her as mine. Wanted to go with her to ensure *Jason* knew she was taken. But I wasn't sure I could go without making an ass out of myself.

Panic emerged and sunk its hooks into me. I was getting

in too deep. Getting attached and jealous and relying on her, which felt disastrously close to relationship territory, and relationships ended in disaster. Sleeping with her was supposed to get her out of my system, but now I wasn't sure that was even possible. Which meant I should... What? Put space between us? Hook up with other girls but not attack guys if Lyla tried to do the same?

"If you're busy tonight, no worries," she said. "I'll definitely want you there when I get the tattoo, though. I'm going to hold onto your hand so tightly that you'll lose circulation—I feel that's only fair since I'll be dealing with the pain of the tattoo."

"Wait? I have to feel pain if you do?"

She nodded. "'Fraid so. It's in the BFF handbook. And besides, you'll probably see it more than anyone else, anyway, so that makes you doubly responsible for helping me through it."

I wanted to be the *only* one who saw it. That was a dangerous line of thinking, though, so I focused on the fact that she'd said *BFF*. It reminded me she didn't want attachments either—it was part of the new her, and the girl was serious about her goals. The panic flooding my system cooled and retreated. Overanalyzing would only ruin everything we had, and what we had was the best of both worlds, so why mess with it?

Not to mention, I needed the friend side of her that knew me better than anyone else right now—more than I ever had. "Do you have any plans for spring break?" I asked.

"My parents hinted they'd like a visit, and apparently Miles is going to be in town—he was so excited our breaks coincided—but all I really want to do is relax." She tugged on my T-shirt, pulling me close, and whispered, "And maybe have lots of sex with this hot guy I know."

First I was going to be Rude Cell Phone Dude in the library, and now I was going to be the sexual deviant walking around with a tent pitched in his pants. I liked her plans for spring break much better than mine. I knew being at home and dealing with everything I needed to would suck, just like I knew there was one thing that'd make it less sucky. "I have to go to New Hampshire."

"Oh. Guess I'll have to find another guy, then." She shrugged, a teasing smile on her face—it better be teasing.

"Not funny." It was as close as I'd get to admitting I didn't want her with anyone else, but hopefully it was enough.

"Maybe I'll drive the three and a half hours home, then." She sighed. "It's the opposite of girl gone wild, but I can't be a party animal all the time, right?"

"Or…" I took her hand and brushed my thumb across the back of it. "You could come with me. I've got to take care of some family crap, but it shouldn't take too much time, and then we could kick back and do the other thing you mentioned."

"You want me to go home with you?"

My heartbeat kicked up a few notches, the panic wedging its way back in. "To hang. Yeah."

"Right. I just meant, you don't usually talk about your family. And you still haven't explained why you might not be coming back next year, and—"

I pressed my mouth to hers, giving her a quick kiss. "Don't make it into a big deal. Just say you'll come."

I could see all the thoughts tumbling through her head, so clear on her face. She wanted to know more than I wanted to tell. Once we were in Canterbury, it's not like I could hide much of anything about my life anymore, but in some ways it'd be easier to just show her. Risky, too, considering my emotions might get the best of me with the constant barrage of memories of my parents, the reality of the situation so close. Still, I'd take her by my side over doing it alone. By the end of dealing with all the decisions I had no idea how to make, I'd need someone to make me laugh and forget about everything else for a while.

"Beck, I..." She exhaled and I prepared myself for her to say no—I'd dealt with it myself this long. Surely I could manage another week. But then she squeezed my hand. "Of course I'll go with you."

Chapter Twenty-Five

LYLA

The world outside the window of Beck's Land Rover had been more greenery than buildings since we'd left Boston, and here and there I got glances of the Merrimack River from the freeway.

I stretched as much as my seat allowed. The trip had flown by, but my legs felt a bit cramped.

"I know just what we need for the last leg of our trip," Beck said, picking up his iPhone and scrolling through his music. The instant the first *bloop* noise started, I grinned. "It's our song!"

As Flo Rida sang the first few lines, I shook my head. "I'm so proud our song is a stripper song."

"Hey, I'd watch your body go down and throw my money around." Beck wrapped his hand around my upper thigh. "I'll swing by the bank. We'll incorporate it into our foreplay."

Tingly heat spread from my stomach outward, the mention of foreplay waking up every cell and sending blips from the times we'd been together dancing through my head. Anytime I thought I was getting in too deep, and that maybe I should stop having sex with him before I ended up irrevocably crushed, I wondered if I could stop even if I tried. Being with Beck was intoxicating—I loved how it made me feel sexy in a way I never had before. How easily he could have me practically panting with a few words or a simple touch. But now there was also the deeper level of intimacy.

It was like my wishful thinking at the party a few weeks ago had come true. He held my hand when we walked across campus together, and we kissed each other hello and good-bye, and everything in between. Despite not being in an official relationship, we spent more time together before and after we had sex, and we'd had some of our deepest conversations lying in his bed, nothing between us.

And the thought of giving it up—giving *him* up—sent pain radiating through my chest.

I told myself we'd still be friends no matter what, so I wouldn't be giving him up completely. But since I'd accidentally fallen head over heels for him, I wasn't sure I could do it. See his perfect messy hair, hear his deep sexy voice, and not want more. Over the past few days I'd told myself of course I loved him. He was my friend—my best friend, really.

But then he'd shoot me a smile, just like he was doing now, and my heart would constrict, and I'd bite back the words that wanted to explode from my mouth. *I love you.*

"You okay?" Beck asked as the song came to a close. He

opened up the console between the seats and held up the Twizzlers and sour gummy worms we'd picked up at the gas station before hitting the road. "More sugar?"

"More sugar. Hmm." I knew it was cheesy, but I leaned over and kissed his cheek. "Don't mind if I do." I ran my lips down to his jaw and kissed my way along the strong line of it and down the column of his neck.

The engine revved as he accelerated. "Twenty more minutes. Then we won't even say hi to my aunt or sister. I'll just carry you inside and have my way with you."

I took the package of sour gummy worms that he'd dropped in his lap when I kissed him, sat back in my seat, and bit into the candy. "Want one?"

He leaned toward me, opening his mouth, and I tossed in a worm. "Thanks, babe."

The breath I sucked in at hearing him call me *babe* was laced with sour sugar, and I started coughing, because I was sexy like that. I reached for my H2O and gulped until the burning subsided.

Beck glanced at me, and I waved him off. "I'm fine. Just…you should really chew instead of inhaling the candy."

"Good tip. I'll keep that in mind."

As we turned off the freeway, a knot formed in my gut. I really had no idea what I was walking in to. While I'd gone on and on about Miles back when we were dating, and mentioned being from New York—but the middle of nowhere part—I supposed that I hadn't been an open book when it came to my family, either. But I was minutes away from meeting his, and there was still so much I didn't know.

I bit my lip. "So, uh…" Finally I decided to stop beating around the bush and say it. "Beck, I feel like I'm going into this situation completely unprepared. I don't even know… how your parents died. Or when. Or pretty much anything other than you've got an aunt and a sister named Megan who was arrested once."

His grip on the steering wheel tightened. "There's not going to be a pop quiz, Lyla."

The words were too sharp. It'd be easy to take offense, but I knew it was more about it being hard for him than being upset with me—I hoped, anyway. "Beck. It's me. I'm not trying to push you. Just trying to know what to say or how to act, and I'd prefer it if I didn't put my foot in my mouth." I reached out and placed my hand on his shoulder, rubbing calming circles with my thumb, the way he often did when we were lying next to each other.

"My parents died in a plane crash early last summer," he said. "Private plane, lots of attention. Everyone wanted a rundown of exactly how the plane crashed, too. They kept asking me how something like that could happen. Like I'd know or want to discuss the gory details."

"I'm sorry." I had to admit there were a lot of questions that came to my mind, too. I guess it's human nature.

"They were coming home from a business trip—ever heard of D&T Pharmaceuticals?"

"Yeah. When I looked up pharmaceutical companies, it was one that I made a note to apply to after I graduated."

"Well, considering it'll be mine when I turn twenty-one, I could probably get you an interview," he said.

I stared at him, sure my mouth was gaping open in the most unattractive way. "*Your* company?"

"My great grandfather Davenport started it—that's where the D comes from. His partner, Mr. Truman, sold his half of the company to my dad a few years ago. Right now the board of directors is running it, but they can't make any big changes without me, even though I don't really have any power for several more months."

"That's…crazy. I mean, huge. I mean…" The plastic bag containing the sour gummy worms crinkled as I fiddled with it, trying to think of what to say to the shocking revelation. "I'm not sure what I mean. It's a lot of information to process."

"You're telling me. Can you really see me in a suit behind a desk?" He brought his fingers up and pressed them into his temple. "Yelling about reports and the bottom line?"

"Is it bad if I say I'd kinda like to see that? Solely for eye candy reasons — you'd look super hot in a suit."

That comment got me a half smile. Then he sighed and glanced at me, anxiety swimming in the blue eyes I'd peered into so many times. "Well, I guess that's good, because that's my future. I've put it off as long as I could, but there are a lot of family and business things I need to deal with this trip. I probably shouldn't have dragged you along, I just…" He turned his palm up and then curled his fingers between mine so that our hands locked together. "I wanted you with me to counteract all the shitty stuff."

I leaned my head on his shoulder. "Then I'm here. For whatever."

He tightened his grip on my hand and kissed my forehead. We passed the rest of the drive in silence, just the occasional squeeze or glance between us, as if we were both checking that the other one was still there.

• • •

"This must be karaoke girl," Megan said after Beck introduced me to his sister—his aunt was apparently due back soon. Like Beck, Megan had a fair complexion, and a hint of strawberry blond showed between her flawless highlights. Her eyes were dark brown, though, and she was on the shorter side.

I glanced at Beck. "You call me karaoke girl?"

"Not me." He tilted his chin at his sister. "Megan does."

"Ever since I called him when you guys were at that karaoke bar. I was like *my brother?* Singing *karaoke?* He must like this girl."

"I do. She's my best friend." Beck flashed me a grin, and I forced a smile onto my lips, trying to be happy enough with that title.

"Let me guess." Megan eyed my blue scoop neck top, multiple beaded necklaces, and long blue and cream skirt. "Art major? No, photography." She pressed her lips into a tight line. "No, I'm sticking with art, but really they both fall into that realm, so either way, I get the points for it."

"Chemistry, actually," I said. "I left the lab coat and goggles at home."

"Though she does manage to look sexy in them," Beck added, hooking his hand on my hip. I wondered if Megan thought his signals about who I was to him were mixed, or if this was normal—maybe all his female "friends" were more like *friends.*

"I'm going to go put our bags away and show Lyla around." Beck shouldered his duffel and gripped the handle of my roller suitcase.

"Mm-hm," Megan said, flopping on the couch and punching on the TV.

With a hand on my back, Beck led me down a giant hall-way—honestly I'd nearly inhaled more sour sugar crystals when we'd pulled up to the large two-story house with tall Victorian columns marking the entryway and a Romeo-and-Juliet-esque balcony off the side. I knew houses like it existed, but I'd never expected to set foot in one.

Beck slipped his thumb underneath the hem of my shirt. "After that discussion back there, I think we better add you wearing a lab coat and nothing else to our list of sex to-dos."

I slowed my pace. "Just remember, you pretty much asked for this."

His eyebrows ticked together.

"Did you hear about the physician and the biologist who went on a date?"

"No," he said, drawing out the word, amusement starting to replace the confusion.

"Think about it. You know the punch line."

The corners of his mouth twitched—he always liked to pretend he was too cool for science jokes, but I knew better.

I turned and ran my finger down his chest. "Say it."

Beck shook his head, the smile he'd been fighting breaking free. "The kinky shit you're into."

I laughed and shoved him. Then, when he still hadn't said anything, I raised my eyebrows and put my hands on my hips.

He sighed. "There was no chemistry."

I clapped and got the crinkly-eyed smile, complete with sexy indention in his cheek. He crooked his finger and I moved closer, wrapping my arms around his waist as he leaned in for a kiss.

"Let's get you into a room and conduct our own

chemistry experiment," he said against my lips. "Or maybe we'll just find a table to bend you over, since chemists do it on a table…periodically."

"Mmm. I love when you talk nerdy to me." I kissed him again, thinking labels didn't matter. Not when we had this.

We climbed up a staircase and turned down another hallway. The bedroom he led me into was about as big as my entire apartment. He set my suitcase at the foot of the king-sized four-poster bed. Was it weird that my mind now went to ways Beck and I could work the bed frame into sex? He was turning me into a one-track-minded girl.

Who was also in love.

Maybe that was making the one-track-mindedness worse.

The strap of Beck's duffel bag slipped down and he hiked it back up. "I'll be just across the hall."

I wanted to ask what the point of that was. He could ask me to come to New Hampshire with him to help him deal with everything, but spending an entire night with me was too much?

Maybe labels do matter. The back and forth when it came to the lines of our relationship were making me feel crazy. Up one minute, down the next. Confident when we were kissing, totally unsure the beat after that.

"Beckett?" A pretty woman with nearly black hair peeked through the open doorway. She came into the room and hugged Beck, then turned to me and extended a hand. "Hi, I'm Tessa Davenport."

She had olive-tone skin, and her eyes were dark like Megan's, which made me wonder what Beck's dad looked like. And what his mom looked like, for that matter. "Lyla Wilder."

Tessa was so flawlessly put together in her wrap dress, glittering jewelry, and heels, I felt like a mess in comparison. "Beckett doesn't usually bring girls home."

I waited for him to insist on the "just friends" aspect again, but he didn't. Maybe that meant I should chime in, but there was something about the factual, toneless way she said it that made it hard for me to know how to respond. I wasn't sure if she thought my being here was a good thing or a bad thing. But with the way she looked me over, a tight smile on her face, I felt like I was on trial.

"Well, it's nice to meet you, Lyla. I was thinking we could all go out for dinner, and then, Beckett"—she turned her sharp gaze on him—"you and I need to sit down and go over a list of action items. It's going to be difficult to fit everything into this week, but hopefully we can at least make a dent in it."

"I'll do my best," Beck said.

"We'll leave in ten, then?"

Beck nodded, and his aunt left the room, her heeled footsteps growing quieter and quieter. He sighed, dropped his duffel bag, and settled onto the bed. "I knew it. She lured me here with talk of one meeting, and now she's going to have me busy every single day. I shouldn't have asked you to come. You'll be so bored."

I climbed onto his lap, straddling him, and brushed my lips over his—it was one of those bold moves I never thought I'd be comfortable doing, but found I couldn't get enough of. "I'll help out however I can, but I've also got books and my computer, with plenty of schoolwork to keep my busy. I'll be fine." I ran my fingers across his jaw, feeling the start of his five o'clock shadow. "They both call you Beckett."

"Yeah, my parents, too—they weren't big fans of the shortened version, actually. But I was always Beck to everyone else."

"So that's what you prefer? Or do I get to call you Beckett sometimes?"

One corner of his mouth twisted up, and then he drew me closer and nipped at my bottom lip. "You, Lyla Wilder, can call me anything you want."

Chapter Twenty-Six

BECK

"You've got to go through their things, Beckett." Aunt Tessa propped her elbows on the large mahogany desk that was more for show than work and put on her serious face which, considering her usual expression was already pretty serious, was quite a feat. "Until you do, I'm afraid you'll never truly move on."

"I've moved on," I retorted. "To another state."

Her forehead tried to furrow, but it was too full of Botox. I loved my aunt, and she was good to take in Megan, but she was more interested in getting back to her "real life," where she didn't have a teenager to take care of, and she could enjoy the money from the business without actually having to work for it. Then again, I was avoiding dealing with the company, so I couldn't really talk.

"I have no idea what to do with everything," I said.

"We need to at least box it up. I can help you later in the week if you'll sort through it and get it labeled. Then, day after tomorrow, I set up a meeting with Mr. Hawthorne. He'll go over any business measures that need your approval, and then you'll meet up with the lawyer who insists his client has an urgent matter she needs to see you about." Tessa rolled her neck from side to side. "You don't have any illegitimate children I should know about, do you?"

"Not that I know of, obviously. But I've always been safe, so I'd be extremely surprised." Of course now she had me thinking of every possible worst-case scenario. I supposed there was that one percent of the time condoms didn't work. But I'd only slept with two girls before college, so the likelihood of one of them coming to me here instead of Boston was slim.

I sat back in the cushy leather chair and pinched the bridge of my nose. Our meeting had already lasted forty minutes, and each thing she'd said only got crappier. I didn't think I could take much more. "Are we done here?"

"For now. As for your guest..."

Every nerve in my body prickled at her tone. "What about her?"

"She's like your mother in a lot of ways. Free spirit with a *cute* style. Intrigued by your wealth and status. I'd hate to see you make the same mistake your father did. We both know how that turned out."

"First of all, Lyla's not like that. This is the first time she's heard about any of this, and she doesn't care about money."

"Oh, Beckett." She gave a what-a-naïve-idiot sigh. "Everyone cares about money."

"Don't worry about Lyla. She's my friend, and she's one

of the best people I've ever met."

"That's exactly what your father said about your mom," Aunt Tessa snarked. I leaned forward in my seat and she held up her hands. "No need to get defensive. I'm sure she's a nice enough girl, but as the only adult in your life, I thought it was my job to tell you to be careful."

"Well, it's not. And my mom made some mistakes, but she wasn't a bad person. If Dad forgave her, you should be able to."

"It was much easier before her lover decided to start visiting her grave all the time. Now their affair is the talk at the club. At the office. I can hardly escape it."

"Just think of my mom. She's dead, and all anyone cares about is who she slept with." I shot out of my chair and stormed out of the room, hot bursts of anger firing through my body. Why didn't people mind their own fucking business? Just because their mistakes weren't broadcast around town, they thought they were better than us.

It wasn't like I hadn't been pissed at Mom for having an affair—there were still days I thought about it and got furious all over again. It wasn't fair for her to expect me to keep it secret, either, and I hated that I ever had. We'd never talked about it—aside from the night when she told me she'd come clean to Dad and swore the affair was over. It wasn't like I wanted to rehash it, but I suppose I'd expected her to apologize. At least she'd apologized to Dad—that was what really mattered. Once, I'd asked him how he could forgive her, and he'd patted me on the shoulder and said, *Son, people make mistakes. When you love someone, there are times you have to be strong and work through issues together, no matter how hard it is.*

I remember thinking it was a crappy deal on his side. That if love meant letting someone betray and hurt you and calling it strong, I'd rather be weak. I wanted to believe Mom had kept her word and that she and Dad were happy there at the end, but I wasn't sure. The one thing I was sure about was that I wanted people to shut the hell up about it.

What I wouldn't give to be in Boston right now, where I could hit the ice, shut out everything else, and get out the aggression suffocating my insides. But since I'd planned on spending my week focused on cardio, I didn't have my gear, and any old skates I could use were at Mom and Dad's. I was already going to have to face the house tomorrow, and I was too exhausted to deal with it tonight.

I glanced at the closed door to my room, thinking I could duck inside and try blasting music to fix my mood. But then I looked at Lyla's door, and my feet automatically moved toward it instead. I lightly knocked and pushed my way inside.

Lyla was asleep on the bed, one of her textbooks open on her chest, her glasses still on. As quietly as possible, I crossed the room, removed the textbook and placed it on the side table, and then reached for her glasses.

The soft sigh that came from her lips made me pause and take her in. Her nose, her perfect lips. The spot in her cheek where the dimple would show up if she smiled. With Aunt Tessa, I felt like I was walking on eggshells. With Megan, I felt the need to be an example and make sure she was taken care of. Even with the guys on the hockey team, I was one of the captains and needed to be a leader.

With Lyla, everything was so easy, no added pressure. Maybe it was a mistake to pull her into this part of my world.

I slid the glasses off her face and she stirred, her eyes fluttering. She reached out and grabbed my hand, pulling me onto the bed next to her.

"Hey," I whispered.

"Mmmm," was her only response as she nuzzled in close, wrapping an arm around my chest and draping one of her legs over my thigh.

Everything seemed better now—like at least I could deal. My eyes drifted closed. I kept thinking I should get up, cover Lyla with a blanket, and go to my room, but I was so comfortable, and she smelled so damn good. So I soaked in how it felt to be next to her, and somewhere along the way, I fell asleep, too.

• • •

"It'll be super boring," I said, flopping onto the bed I'd left around three a.m., when I realized I'd accidentally spent most of the night with Lyla. It'd taken every ounce of energy I had to force myself away from her and into my cold, empty bed, and now I was thinking I was stupid for not staying and waking up next to her. Maybe I could've even joined her in the shower.

"Not if you're there." Lyla wrapped a scarf around the top of her head, knotted it, and slid it around so that the material made a headband, the ends of it mixing in with her red waves. "And definitely not if I'm there."

True. But what if I started crying like a baby? Then I'd never be able to look her in the eye again. Still, Megan was off with friends, and while Tessa was home, after what she'd said yesterday, I didn't exactly want Lyla to be alone with her. I stood and extended my hand. "Let's do this, then."

On the drive, as if she sensed I needed a mood lightener, Lyla sang along with the radio, the wrong lyrics coming out of her mouth about fifty percent of the time, as usual. When I teased her about it, she said, "The words I put in are way more interesting. You should be thanking me, not mocking me."

"Is that right?"

"Totally." Her eyes widened as we drove up to the tall, wrought iron gate. I punched in the code and pulled up to the house, trying to push away the unease crawling up my spine. "And I thought your aunt's place was enormous."

Tessa had asked me if I wanted to put it on the market—she complained that she was still paying the groundskeeper and maid service, and it was a huge waste. I told her to stop then, and I'd get it fixed up if and when I moved back in. Apparently it was ridiculous to let it get run-down, too, because then what would people think?

"I don't deserve it," I said as I took it in, the three expansive stories with the large paved driveway and manicured lawn.

Lyla turned in her seat to face me. "What does that mean?"

"Nothing." I parked and started out of the car, but she grabbed my arm.

"Nope. You've got to explain now. Don't make me start with the chemistry jokes or the cat pictures, because I'll use cruel and unusual punishments to get you to talk. You know I will."

Despite the situation, I cracked a smile. Then I leaned back in my seat. "People used to tell me that I was lucky.

I got whatever I wanted, whether I deserved it or not. The fact is, it's true. The only thing I worked really hard for was hockey, because I loved it, and all I ever wanted was to play for the Bruins. I worked for my grades, too, but only because Mom threatened to not let me play hockey if they slipped. But honestly, even they came pretty easily to me." I glanced across the Land Rover at Lyla. "So now I own this huge house I don't need, and I'm going to have an extremely successful company just handed over to me, and I *want* to deserve it."

"But?"

"But I'm not sure I even want any of it." I curled my hand around the bill of my hat, messing with it to give my hands something to do. "It'd probably be easy enough to hire someone to do my dad's old job, but I feel like I'd be disappointing him. Working with him and then eventually taking over was always his dream for me."

"You can't live your entire life for someone else, though," she said.

I let that hang in the air, trying to comfort myself with the idea. Unfortunately, it didn't take away the guilt filling me at the thought of not taking over the company. "I'm willing to work hard, but I'm having trouble letting go of playing for the NHL. Which is probably just a dream anyway. I could give up my position in the company, work my ass off at hockey for two years, and still not make it."

The truth slammed into me, and the spark of hope that maybe I could keep playing snuffed out. "No, I can't risk it. What would I do for work, then? Who'd take care of Megan? Who'd make sure my family's company runs the way my dad would've wanted it to?"

Lyla placed her hand over mine. "That's a lot of pressure to put on yourself, Beck. Maybe you'll find that you like working for the company, but I'm afraid that running it with no passion for it, or having to always wonder *what if*, is going to make you despise it. I'm sure that's not what your dad would've wanted. Your sister obviously loves you and wants you to be happy, and I bet she'd want you to follow your dream as much as I do. That said, you're more than just a hockey player, so if it doesn't work out, it's not like you're not good at other things. And honestly, I think you should at least finish college either way. Give yourself more options. But maybe that's because I've been preached to about getting a degree since I was five or so."

"But your goal is to end up with a coveted spot in a company that will basically land in my lap. Even if you get promoted every few years, you'll work your ass off and still only make a fraction of what I do. Doesn't that make you hate me a little?"

"Now, what good would that do?" She laced her fingers with mine. "Maybe if I didn't know you, it'd be easy to think that way. I'm sure your father worked hard, and I'm sure that whichever career you choose, you'll throw yourself into it."

"It's the choosing that's hard."

"Duh, that's life."

I raised an eyebrow at her. "Duh?"

"You heard me." She ran her fingers up my arm, and then they were drifting up, into the hair at the base of my neck—I could get lost in her touch. Just close my eyes and never deal with anything again. "When I look at you, you know what I see?"

I met her gaze, finding it suddenly hard to breathe.

"I see the guy who saw me when no one else did," she said. "That's what matters to me. That's who you are. Not this house or your dad's company, but a good guy who's been there for me since I first met you."

My heart expanded, pressing against my ribcage. "Anyone who doesn't see you is an idiot, Lyla."

I cupped her chin, tipping her face up so I had better access to her lips. Then I kissed her. It started out soft, but grew in urgency, her taking over one moment, and then me taking the lead the next. Back and forth, until she ended up on top of me, and the temperature in the car shot to sizzling.

As I peered into her eyes, at the green and the brown battling it out for control, I found myself wanting to take that next step with Lyla. If I did believe in relationships and love, Lyla would be the perfect girlfriend. Being with her like this made me want to take a risk. Make that leap of faith.

And as she slowly lowered her mouth to mine again, I decided that for her, maybe I could.

Chapter Twenty-Seven

Lyla

Beck didn't say much as we went through the rooms of the house, each of them stunning and richly decorated. Not that he seemed to notice or care. His movements were mechanical, precise, and carefully devoid of emotion. But I could feel everything he was holding back, as if it were a living, breathing entity that wanted to wrap its arms around Beck and hold him down until he cracked.

As he sorted the things he wanted to keep from the items Tessa would have movers come in and box up, I helped the best I could. Mostly by keeping the music going and chatting about classes or cats or movies or basically anything I could think of so the silence didn't overwhelm either one of us. Twice Beck had told me he needed to go check on something, and the thickness in his voice told me he was struggling with his emotions.

When we took a late lunch break that probably was closer to dinner, I noticed the large cement court with netted goals on either end. It looked out of place compared to the flowers, shaped hedges, and large pool. "Did you play street hockey, too?"

Beck came up behind me and put his hand on my back, his gaze focused on the court through the patio doors. "When I wasn't on the ice, I played street hockey. I knew I needed to practice as much as possible if I wanted to be good enough to compete at the college level. I think I spent more time out there than in here, actually."

I twisted to face him. "Let's play."

"Hockey?"

I nodded, excitement bubbling up—this was what we both needed. "Ice hockey intimidates me—I've only ice skated a couple of times—but when it comes to rollerblades, I'm pretty good." I frowned. "Of course, I didn't think of bringing them with me."

"I bet Megan has some in her closet. If you really want to play."

"I think we need a break. And what better way to get that, than for me to beat you at hockey on your own court?"

Beck grinned—the first real grin I'd seen since we'd stepped foot in the house. He took my hand and led me to Megan's room. We found a pair of skates that were a bit tight in the toes, but not so much I couldn't make do, and then we headed down the hall.

"Ooh, I can't believe I'm in Beckett Davenport's bedroom," I said as we stepped through the doorway. "If these walls could talk…" Suddenly I realized I might not want to know what they'd say. *Way to go, Lyla. Make him happy and then immediately go into awkward land.*

But Beck just smiled at me from his crouched position in front of his closet. "You're the only girl I've ever brought in here, actually. There was a rule about no members of the opposite gender in the bedroom. My mom spent a lot of time helping run a charity for low-income families in Concord during the day, as well as plenty of time at the spa, shopping, and going to lunches, but she always made sure to be here when Megan and I got home from school. Mostly she was in her office, focused on her laptop, but she had this freaky sixth sense when it came to knowing I had a girl over and was thinking of breaking the rule."

He seemed to be lost in reverie for a moment, but then his eyes refocused, the happiness in his features fading quickly. He returned his attention to the closet, so I took the chance to look around and see if I could figure out what high-school-Beck was like.

Hockey posters lined the walls—no surprise there. I leaned closer to the two framed pictures on the dresser. A team photo with Beck in the middle, his cute face easy to spot in the crowd, and one of him alone in his uniform, early high school years from the looks of it. His grin showed off braces.

"Just when I'd come up with the perfect plan to sneak in my girlfriend so we could"—Beck made air quotes—"'take things to the next level,' she decided to leave me for Dale Buchanan. He played polo."

I turned away from the line of trophies I was studying. "Polo? Is that supposed to be more impressive than hockey?"

"Apparently it's classier."

Beck came up with a pair of skates and two hockey sticks. I stared at my hockey player boyfriend—er, friend—and tried to imagine him playing polo instead. I'm sure it was a fine game and all, but it wasn't my Beck. And regardless of labels, he was mine. "Clearly, she was an idiot. I prefer guys with scars and imminent teeth loss in their future."

Beck flashed his perfect pearly whites at me. "I'll see about knocking one out next game." Then the same misery-filled expression he'd had in the car when he'd talked about giving up hockey returned.

"College or not, you've got to keep playing. However you can." I took his hand and squeezed it. "Promise me."

"I'm playing now, aren't I?"

"Yes, but I'm suggesting a league where you might win once in a while."

His laugh echoed through me, leaving me so happy I practically skipped down the stairs. Within a few minutes, we stood across from each other on the cement hockey court, a puck between the hockey sticks in our hands.

I was pretty sure I was about to make a fool of myself, but the thing about embarrassing yourself a lot is you get a little numb to it. Plus, Beck already knew I was coordinationally challenged.

"Go!" I shouted, and slapped at the puck. I took off after it, Beck right next to me. We skated back and forth, the hockey sticks crashing as we fought for the puck. Beck got control and blocked every one of my attempts to steal it. Damn boy and his skills. I skated backward, waiting to make my move. When he lifted his stick, readying to take a swing for a goal, I flew forward and slammed my body into his, thinking I'd impress him with my checking skills.

Only then I was falling back, dropping my stick to grasp at air. Beck caught my arm just before I went down, making me land with more of an easy skid on my butt than a tail-bone-fracturing slam—good thing I'd worn jeans today.

He hovered over me. "You okay?"

I groaned. "You couldn't have wobbled a little?"

"I'm sorry. I'm so used to catching the impact—that *was* an impact, right?"

I slapped his arm, and he laughed before yanking me to my feet.

"Your skating is truly impressive, though. Didn't expect it, Wilder." He punctuated the statement with a smack on the butt. Guess he thought he'd give me the full jock experience. He retrieved the puck and batted it back and forth with his stick. "Ready for round two?"

It took me five attempts, and I suspected Beck didn't pursue the fast break quite as hard as he could've, but I finally managed to send one into the goal. I threw my hands up in the air and screamed, that loud victory yell that I'd heard sporty type people do but never had much use for.

Beck scooped me up and spun me around.

I clung to him, wrapping my arms tightly around his neck. "Don't drop me, okay?"

"What do you think I am? An amateur?" He skated over to the edge of the court and slowly set me down, his hands lingering on the sides of my waist. "Thanks, Ly. I needed that."

My heart turned over in my chest. "Me, too." I shook my bangs out of my eyes. "So, whaddya think? Do I have a future in the NHL?"

"Yes." He pulled me against him and lowered his mouth to mine, teasing my lips with his tongue. "Maybe just on the sidelines, cheering me on, though."

It was an offhand comment, but it was talk of the future, and it sent a spark of hope through me. Surely I wasn't the only one who was falling. Even if he wasn't in love with me yet, I'd take the possibility of it.

His phone rang and he dug it out, keeping his other hand on the curve of my butt. He muttered a few answers and then looked at me and said, "Actually, don't worry about us for dinner. I think Lyla and I are going to stay here tonight."

He rolled his eyes. "I know, Aunt Tessa. I'll be there." Pause. "I have an alarm on my phone, and I've managed to get to places on time by myself for years. I'm sure."

When he hung up, he smiled at me, and the tenderness in his eyes stole the breath from my lungs. "I hope you're okay with staying here overnight. Seems sad for my bedroom to never see any action." He pushed his fingers through my hair and wrapped his hand around my neck, his thumb resting over my rapidly accelerating pulse point. "Plus, I want to spend an entire night with you lying next to me."

I tipped onto my toes and pressed my lips to his, thinking *It's happening! It's happening!* "Sounds perfect."

. . .

The darker it got, the quieter Beck was, and I worried he'd regretted the decision to stay. But when I asked, he insisted he was fine. He instructed me to pick out a movie from the large entertainment center while he went to get something to drink.

Twenty minutes later, he still hadn't come back. It was a big house, but twenty minutes was a stretch, so I went to look for him.

I found him in the downstairs office, sitting in the chair behind the desk, his head in his hands. "Beck?" I took a cautious step inside, not wanting to interrupt, but unable to leave him like that.

He looked up when I touched his shoulder, the sorrow on his face so raw it punched me in the chest. "Sorry. I… This was my mom's office. I stepped inside to… I don't even know."

Papers were scattered across the desk and the drawers hung open. I hadn't gotten a good look at the room when I passed by it on the way back and forth to the kitchen, but I didn't think it'd been messy. "Were you looking for something?"

Beck pinched the bridge of his nose. "I wanted to see if my mom was still having an affair. I don't know what I thought she'd have here to prove if she was or wasn't, but…" He gestured vaguely at the desk and exhaled a shaky breath.

What do you say to something like that? "You think she had an affair?"

"No, I know she did. Sophomore year I ditched my last class of the day because I'd accidentally grabbed two left skates and didn't want to be late for practice. When I came home, I heard my mom in the office and thought I'd say hi. But when I pushed open the door, she was in here with Mr. Brooks, my dad's financial advisor who also helped with the charity she was involved in. They weren't having sex, thank God, but it was clear they were about to."

"That…*sucks*." It wasn't nearly strong enough, or probably helpful, but it was all I had.

Beck sniffed and shook his head. "Sorry. I thought I'd dealt with it, but apparently I just held it at bay long enough for it to come crashing into me at the worst possible time." He pulled the brim of his hat lower and stood. "Ignore me. Let's go watch the movie."

I placed my hand on the center of his chest, stopping him from moving around me. "Remember how you once said that with me, you could just be you?" I asked, and he nodded. "Well, you can be. Be sad. Be mad. Be whatever the hell you're going to be. You don't have to hide it from me. There's nothing you could say that would scare me away or make me think less of you."

The muscles in his jaw flexed like he was trying to hold back. I reached up and smoothed a finger over them. His mask slowly cracked and his shoulders slumped. "My dad forgave her and moved on," he said. "Why can't I?"

"It's not an easy thing to forgive. I'm not sure I could do it."

Beck stared at me for what seemed like forever, and for a moment I thought he was going to confess to cheating on me. Which, well, he couldn't have. Not really. But it'd still hurt like hell if he told me he'd been hooking up with other people on the side, especially during the past few weeks when we'd grown even closer.

"It doesn't help that, according to the rumors, it was still going on," he said. "And I have no idea if it's true or not. But it's possible, so then I get pissed off she'd betray my dad like that again—that she did it in the first place—and then I feel like shit because I'm thinking badly about my dead mother. Every good memory is taken over by it, and I…" His voice broke and he looked away.

I wrapped my arms around him, wanting to hold him tightly until he felt whole again. I opened my mouth to try to come up with something to say, but then he whispered, "Make it go away, Lyla."

Of all the kisses we'd shared, none of them had gone so slowly. Or felt so sweet. This one was different, like he was transferring part of himself to me. I took it in, hoping it meant I could take away the pain and help him escape. We stumbled out of the room, our mouths and bodies never breaking contact.

At the base of the curving marble staircase, I peeled off his shirt. I lost mine halfway up. My bra hit the floor at the top, and by the time we got to the bedroom, all I had on were the pair of tiny lacy panties I'd worn hoping Beck and I would get a chance to be alone. When Beck moved toward the bed, I pulled back. He wanted it to go away—I planned on making sure he wasn't thinking about anything but me.

He groaned as I slowly kissed and licked my way down his body, his muscles twitching under my mouth. I'd hesitated to do this before, and Beck never pushed it. I used to think blow jobs were slightly demeaning, the whole down-on-your-knees, could-be-anyone thing. For the first time I got that it was caring about someone else more than yourself, and that made it unexpectedly hotter than I ever could've imagined.

Empowerment filled me. I could be the one to make up for everything wrong in his life. I'd stay by his side, no matter what, and eventually he'd see it was all going to be okay. It was scary to give him so much of myself, but at least I knew Beck would take care of it.

Chapter Twenty-Eight

I waited for the sharp edge of panic to set in, but as I looked at Lyla, my lungs didn't constrict the way they did for a moment last night during my confession in the office, when I wondered if I was letting her in too much.

The woman completely unraveled me, and I didn't care to be wound back up and put in a box where I had to be careful about everything I did or said. I ran my fingers across her bare back, grinning when I hit a ticklish spot and she jerked, pressing her breasts into me with the movement. "Morning."

She tipped her head up and flashed me a beautiful smile I vowed to capture on my phone so I could stare at it whenever I had a crappy day.

"Breakfast?" I linked my fingers with hers and kissed the top of her head. "We'll go out—I won't even demand you make me pancakes."

"Damn right you won't."

I chuckled and glanced at the time. "We better get going, though. I've got to get to my lawyer's office in Concord by eleven. So we'll do breakfast in yesterday's walk-of-shame clothes, and then we can go get cleaned up. After that, you'll have time to hang out at my aunt's and study, or if you want, you can take the Land Rover and explore. I could just call when I need you to pick me up." Or, I supposed I could take one of the other cars out of the garage, but that'd mean not riding with Lyla this morning, and I wasn't ready to let her go yet, even for a few minutes.

Yep, I've definitely reached sappy territory. But I didn't care.

She pulled on my T-shirt and went in search of her clothes. Separating at the end of the day like we'd been doing all this time was stupid. Pointless.

Lyla came back in fully dressed—a shame, that whole wearing-clothes thing—and tossed me my shirt. She twisted her hair into a bun and glanced around. I grabbed a pen out of the cup on my desk and tossed it to her.

"Thanks." Once her bun was secured, she placed her hand on my chest, leaned in, and kissed me. "I just wanna say that I'm glad you saw my list, and I'm glad taking care of lucky number seven made us grow closer instead of apart. I was so scared it was going to screw everything up."

"Me, too. It's why I tried so hard to resist when I first started thinking about it." I curled my hand around her bare neck. "But now that I know how amazing this can be, you're never getting rid of me."

Her beautiful lips curved into a smile and my heart lurched. "I'm holding you to that."

As we drove through town, I felt peace like I hadn't experienced in months. I didn't even care if we ran into anyone I knew, or what questions they might ask—none of it mattered right now. Not with Lyla with me. When we got to the café, we loaded up on pancakes, eggs, and bacon.

At Aunt Tess's, we split for showers. As soon as I was dressed, I found Lyla in her room, her hair wet and her clothes still clinging to her damp skin. "Babe, I need to go or I'll be late. You want the car?"

"No, I'll be fine here." She moved over to me and threw her arms around my neck. "But hurry back, because I'll miss you." She pressed her lips to mine. "I'm trying"—kiss—"to not get carried away with the mushy stuff here"—another string of short kisses that merged into the next—"But I already can't wait for whatever we do tonight."

"If this is carried away, I say go for it." I grinned as she kissed one cheek and then the other, then the side of my mouth, before placing her lips on mine again. "Tell you what, I still owe you a movie. We'll order whatever horrific chick flick you want and have ice cream."

She ran her tongue across my bottom lip and then gently sucked on it. A jolt of heat tore through me, revving me up to fully aroused in two seconds flat.

I groaned. "I really have to go."

"Okay," she said, but she wrapped her arms tighter around me. Another kiss and we ended up on the bed—that one was on me, but considering the wicked things she was doing with her tongue, I couldn't help but respond in kind. While I usually preferred to take my time, the way we had last night, we ended up racing though sex. Fast and furious, a blur of skin-on-skin, moans, panted breaths, and then coming together.

Head still spinning, I gave her one last kiss, reluctantly forced myself to my feet and dressed, and then raced out of the house. Tessa would kill me if she found out I was late. *Worth it,* I thought as I peeled out of the driveway, my lips stretched in a grin. At least no matter what happened, Lyla would be here at the end of the day to make it all seem better.

I think this is what being in love feels like.

• • •

The dark-haired woman who sat across the conference table from Mr. Hawthorne and me looked to be in her early thirties. There was something about the way she studied me that made apprehension prickle across my skin.

Her lawyer—Mr. Smith—sat in the chair next to her. "Son, I'm sorry for your loss, and I wish there was a better time to do this, but Ms. Walker can't wait any longer. She has a daughter to take care of, and that has to be her top priority right now."

"I really am sorry," Ms. Walker said, her green-eyed gaze on me, and Mr. Smith shot her a stern look that made me think she wasn't supposed to talk.

I folded my arms on the polished table. "What's this all about? Just spit it out so I can get to the other matters I need to take care of today." The words didn't sound like mine. Me, an uptight businessman who didn't have time for small talk. But after two hours with Mr. Hawthorne, sorting through estate paperwork and D&T "action items" I barely understood, I was actually starting to feel like I fit the part.

Mr. Smith set his pen on the table and steepled his hands under his chin. "Your father had another child. With Ms. Walker."

Another child? My mind revolted at the words; my lungs turned to stone. I glanced at Ms. Walker and her face crumpled.

"Is this supposed to be funny? Some attempt to extort money from the company?" Anger rose, burning hotter and hotter by the second. "Going after a dead man's family is low."

Ms. Walker burst into tears, and Mr. Smith put his hand on her shoulder. "I assure you, it's not a joke, and we're not trying to go after your family. Only trying to get what's owed to my client and the child. Richmond Davenport made monthly payments that helped Ms. Walker take care of their daughter. But he didn't add them to his will, and with him gone, the payments have stopped. His daughter deserves the same comfort his legitimate children have. I believe he would've wanted it that way."

Everything inside me was crumbling. The room was too hot and too cold and the walls were closing in on me. *Mom* was the cheater. Dad… I curled my hands into fists, fighting the urge to flip the table and throw one of the million pretentious chairs lining it out the window. He wasn't like that. Our family was healing. Coming back together.

I heard his words in my head again and again: *Son, people make mistakes. When you love someone, there are times you have to be strong and work through issues together, no matter how hard it is.*

So much for working through issues. So much for fucking love.

"Beckett, you should know that your father always spoke so highly of you." Ms. Walker gave me a watery smile and dabbed her eyes with a tissue. "I wish we'd met under other circumstances, but now that we have, I'd love for you to meet your sister. For us to get to know one another."

How could she sit there and act like she wasn't ruining everything? "Do you have proof? Any proof at all? Besides that he gave you money?"

Mr. Hawthorne put a hand on my shoulder—apparently it was the go-to lawyer calm down tactic—but it was going to take a lot more than that to stop the rage coursing through my body. "Let's hear them out, and then we'll decide what to do."

The details slowly spilled out. The *baby* was six years old. I did the math every way possible, and it always meant that Dad cheated on Mom *before* she had her affair. I wondered if it was why she'd turned to Mr. Brooks. Did she know about the other woman? The child? She must've.

But why didn't she say anything—I wouldn't have been so hard on her.

I closed my eyes, thinking of how far apart we'd grown after that. All that time I'd never get back, robbed from me because of the lies. Regret and shame swelled, gutting me from the inside out. Before they'd finished with me, a viscous wave of truth hit me: our family's name had already been dragged through the mud, and it was about to get worse. There was no way this wouldn't get out. I didn't even care about the money. Everyone would know that my parents slept around, the entire town would be buzzing about the love child, not satisfied until they'd squeezed every drop of evil gossip out of the scandal. Megan would flip out and spiral out of control again, and I didn't know what to do.

Ms. Walker was full on crying now, tears streaming down her cheeks. "He loved me, and I loved him, and he loved our daughter. We were supposed to be together, but he was waiting for Megan to graduate, and now we'll"—she sniffed and the sobbing escalated—"never have the chance."

I stared at her tear-streaked face, completely numb. Love. What a load of shit. I remembered the way Mom used to tell her and Dad's love story, so similar to the one Ms. Walker was blubbering about.

None of it mattered. Regardless of how good it was at the beginning, it ended with the search for more. Someone else more attractive. More money. More power. Control.

That was my legacy.

Earlier today, I'd had a moment where I thought love was more than just four little letters people threw around. Something powerful and real that could heal the past through acceptance and understanding.

What a fucking idiot. The only power it had was to take people at their most vulnerable, hurt them, and wear them down until all that was left were shattered hearts and ruined lives.

Chapter Twenty-Nine

Lyla

"Wow," I said after I was sure Tessa was gone. "She doesn't seem to like me very much." Her words were nice, all the right ones strung politely together, but a chill emanated from her every time she looked my way. As soon as I'd finished my lunch, I'd wanted to flee the dining room, but waiting at least a few minutes after my last bite seemed like the polite thing to do. When she'd said she needed to run errands and excused herself, I'd let out a relieved breath.

Megan lowered the phone she'd been texting on. "Aunt Tessa's not what you'd call a 'people person.' Now you see what I have to deal with every day. Only add a dramatic sigh as she mumbles, 'I never wanted kids.'"

"Ouch."

Megan shrugged as if she didn't care, but I could see the pain carefully held under the surface—it was the same expression I occasionally saw on Beck.

"I'm sure people tell you that they're sorry about your parents a lot, but I truly am sorry," I said. "I can't even imagine how hard it'd be to deal with."

"It was really bad right after, but at least I had Beckett to talk to—or more like we'd distract each other from moping around. It sucked, but I thought maybe eventually we'd be okay. Then he was gone, too, and…" Megan dropped her gaze to her empty plate and shook her head.

I didn't know what to say. Obviously she'd felt abandoned, and I even understood why she might lash out. If Beck decided to ignore me, I could only imagine what lengths I'd go to get his attention. "If it makes you feel any better, I can tell every time it's you on the phone. His whole face lights up and his voice goes soft—he'd deny it, I'm sure, because he'd say he's far too manly and tough for that, but trust me, it's true."

A smile broke through, taking the edge off the grief that'd been filling Megan's features. "Well, I can tell when he's with you, too—he does things like karaoke. Plus, he likes to keep his college life and his life here completely separate, and he still totally brought you here, which is, like, *huge*. He used to always tell me love was crap, and that I should be careful, because guys were big jerks who just wanted to use me—like, he'd stare down boys who tried to talk to me. Seriously, *so* embarrassing. But when you guys got here, I knew he'd changed his mind—it's written across his face every time he looks at you. He's crazy in love with you."

"Oh, I don't know if he's quite there." The words beckoned to me, though, tingly hope buzzing through my chest. Time for a reality check before my emotions got too carried away. "He still introduces me as his friend, after all. I think I'm in crazy-in-love land by myself."

Immediately, I worried I'd said too much. What if it came back to bite me? Not to mention I probably should've told him I loved him before telling his sister—if I wasn't scared it'd freak him out and send him running.

Megan waved off my comment. "I know my brother. You've got nothing to worry about."

Last night and this morning, it *had* felt like everything had changed. What was going on between us was definitely more than sex. More than friendship.

"Thanks," I said. "I needed to hear that."

"Sure thing." Megan pushed out from the table. "Want to see what's on TV?"

Studying would be the responsible thing to do—I liked to be ahead instead of behind, and with my list—and Beck—taking up so much time, I was falling more on the behind side of the line. My history test hadn't gone so well last week, and if I didn't ace my next test in there and my lit class, I'd be screwed. Without my scholarship, I couldn't afford next semester. But the teenage girl I'd expected to be totally uninterested in me wanted to hang out. After seeing how lonely she was, I couldn't say no.

So I followed her to her room, where she had a cushy loveseat and a big-screen TV. We kicked back and she flipped through channels, watching about half the time and chatting the rest. The more we talked, the more I liked her. She was funny and could talk for several minutes straight without taking a breath, and I loved every second of it.

It did make me wonder if Beck should be closer to her, though. She needed someone who'd build her up when she was feeling down, set boundaries when she was feeling rebellious, and pay attention to her so she didn't feel so alone. I just wished I knew a way for him to be close to his family, not feel so burdened by the company, and play hockey in Boston, where he'd also be with me. Was that really so much to ask?

...

Tessa had invited me to go with her and Megan to dinner, but I'd declined, wanting to be at the house when Beck got back. I'd texted him a couple of times, asking how it was going and if he was nearly done, but so far, no answer.

So I'd set up camp on the silky floral couch with gilded trim that kept catching my hair. I lifted my giant literature book higher, trying to focus on the paragraph I'd read three times without knowing what it said. My mind kept replaying talking to Megan and everything she'd said about Beck and how she could tell he'd changed his mind.

If he didn't feel what I'm feeling, he never would've opened up to me the way he did yesterday, I'm sure of it.

If anything, yesterday was another reason to let him know how much I cared. Let him know he didn't have to go through things alone anymore. My pulse raced faster and faster as I seriously considered telling him I loved him. Honestly, I wasn't sure how much longer I could hold it back. It was dying to burst out of me, to spread the warmth and happiness radiating through every inch of my body.

Just do it. Be bold.

That was the whole point of the bucket list, right? Stop holding back. Take risks. And how many times had I told

Whitney to stop driving herself crazy and talk to Matt already? Still, it was a hell of a risk.

With a hell of an awesome payback if he felt the same way.

I'm going to do it. Nerves rolled through my stomach. *I'm going to tell him I love him.*

I heard the front door open and tossed my book onto the coffee table. I barely restrained myself from running.

Beck was turned, pulling the door closed behind him. A thrill shot through me at the sight of him.

"Hey! How'd it—" The tension filling every inch of his rigid posture and tight expression as he spun to face me stopped me cold. Dark circles showed under his eyes and his hair was messy, like he'd been repeatedly running his hands through it. "What happened? Are you okay?"

"No, I'm not okay."

I moved to hug him, but he held out an arm, keeping me back. "Just…don't."

Hurt flooded my chest. "What's going on?"

"My dad has another kid. He had an affair, too, just like my mom. Because that's what my family does. And now I get to clean up the mess."

"I'm so sorry. I—"

"I can't be with you, Lyla. Not the way you want."

Panic rose up, its steel fingers clutching my heart as I struggled to keep up with the change in topic. "Wait. How'd we go from talking about your parents to you and me?" I took a step toward him and put my hand on his arm. "We can deal with this. Together."

Beck shook his head. "I'll just let you down. You need to find someone else."

No matter how much I tried to breathe in, I couldn't get any oxygen to my lungs. "I don't want anyone else."

"You wanna wait until I cheat on you?" he asked, his words as sharp as ice picks.

Tears crawled up my throat and blurred my eyes. "That's crap, and a total cop-out. You can control who you sleep with. When you love someone, you work at it. Don't use your parents as an excuse to dump me."

"In order to dump you, I'd have to be dating you. I told you from the beginning that all this could be was sex—I warned you."

"You did." My chin trembled, my voice along with it. "How silly of me to go and fall in love with you anyway."

He stared at me, his blue eyes so cold and hard. Cracks formed in my heart, pain pushing in and pouring out at the same time.

"It's not real, Ly. I pretended I could be a normal guy with a girlfriend, and you pretended to be the sexy party girl. But at the end of the day, we were both lying."

My tears spilled over and ran down my cheeks. "That's me." I sniffed. "Pretend sexy, and in love with a guy who doesn't feel the same way." I strode toward the door, surprised my body still functioned despite the crushing agony obliterating my internal organs. Right before I stepped outside, I turned back and looked at my supposed best friend. "Thanks for the mind-blowing sex at least. So glad you took pity on the plain girl who couldn't get off."

Chapter Thirty

The bang of the door slamming behind her echoed through my body. Loud. Empty. Hollow.

Her face. The pain. My lungs felt like they were collapsing in on themselves, squeezing out every bit of air until no more remained.

I told myself it'd be better for her in the end—I couldn't pull her into my toxic life. After this semester, there'd be no more college or hockey for me. I needed to take care of this giant shitstorm. Find a way to tell Megan she had a half sister out there, and talk to Aunt Tessa so we could figure out if we should try to keep it quiet or be in control of it coming out the way we wanted it to.

There'd be no more laid back nights with Lyla, pretending my life was something it wasn't. I ran shaky fingers over my forehead. I wanted to run after her and make sure she at least knew she wasn't plain—she was sexy and beautiful and full of life, and I couldn't slowly ruin her one mistake at a time. But how was I supposed to talk to her after what'd just happened?

Still, I had to go after her. She didn't have her suitcase or a car, and I didn't want her walking the road alone.

Shit, this is going to suck.

I'd meant to ease into the conversation, but how big of a jackass would I be if I kissed her and pretended we were okay, only to pull the rug out from under her when she fell that much harder? Losing the right to kiss her and have her in my bed made my bones ache, but even deeper under that was the acidic knowledge I'd also wrecked our friendship. One of the most important things in my life, and honestly, the main reason I'd survived this past year.

Megan burst through the door, her jaw set and her eyebrows in an angry V. "What the hell did you do?"

"I…" I shook my head. I had no words, no desire to make up a lame excuse. "Is she okay?"

"No. She was walking down the road, crying, Beckett! Aunt Tessa's giving her a ride somewhere. I tried to get her to stay, but that only made her cry harder, and Aunt Tessa sent me inside." Megan crossed her arms. "Start talking."

"You're just a kid. You wouldn't understand."

"Just a kid? Well, at least I know that you'll never meet anyone better than Lyla, and if you let her go, you're an idiot. Pretty sure that makes me smarter than you, regardless of my age." She stormed past me in a huff—so now all the women in my life hated me. Great.

I walked into the living room, sat down on the couch, and ran my hands through my hair. *Maybe…* I thought of Mom and Dad and the counseling they'd done so we could be a big happy lie. Even if I could get my shit together, I needed to face the facts. My time in Boston was almost up, and most of it was going to be filled with practice, playoffs, and with any luck, the Frozen Four. What was I going to do? Try to fix a relationship that'd end in two months anyway? Why draw out the pain?

So much damn pain—it felt like I'd been steamrolled by a Zamboni. If it already hurt this badly, how much worse would another couple months of holding on and getting that much closer only to separate again hurt? Not like she'd take me back after what I said, anyway.

I lay back and closed my eyes, not even bothering to move when the stupid trim of the floral headache couch dug into my skull. I wanted everything to go away. But since there wasn't a skating rink nearby—I doubted hockey would even help right now, anyway—and Lyla was long gone, the suffocating pain of missing her, on top of missing my parents while being angry at both of them, just came rushing at me that much faster.

• • •

I'd put off doing this the entire week, but it was time to suck it up. All I did these days was go to class, go to practice, and return to my empty, depressing-as-hell apartment. Everywhere I looked I saw the lack of Lyla—the giant missing gap in my life. She wasn't on the couch, insisting on a chick flick. No one texted me cat pictures or smiley faces. There were no cheesy chemistry jokes, complete with the sound of her laughter. My sheets even smelled like her, but she wasn't there, either, and when I washed them to get rid of her perfume, the absence of her scent depressed me even more.

I knocked on her apartment door. I heard shuffling behind the mock wood. "Lyla, I just came to bring you your stuff. And to see if—"

The door swung open and Whitney stood there, a scowl on her face. "What do you want, asshat?"

"I-Is she okay?"

"No, she's not *okay*. She's the nicest girl I know, and you broke her heart."

I leaned against the frame, trying to come up with something good to say. I wanted to let everything spill out—how much I missed her. How I should've told her she was perfect and sexy and the smartest person I knew. That I was drowning without her, and for the first time in my life, I got why they called it a broken heart, because all mine did was sit in my chest and ache with each beat.

Not even hockey helped, and I'd been playing like shit, to the point where Coach asked me if I wanted to sit the bench during regionals. I'd barely bit back saying that it didn't matter anymore.

Whitney eyed the box in my hand. I'd overnighted Lyla's suitcase and books to the apartment since I knew she'd stress about it. But because her literature book wasn't with the rest of her things, it'd gotten left behind, and I'd found a few of her belongings at my apartment. A scarf, a pair of earrings, a couple of movies, and half a dozen girly pens and pencils she probably could do without but seemed like a shame to throw away—how'd she secure her bun without them?

Honestly, I could've shipped this box, too, but I needed to know if Lyla was okay. I knew it'd hurt to see her, but I figured it couldn't hurt much worse, so I might as well shut off the constant curiosity.

Whitney yanked the box out of my hand. "Go before she comes back. Seeing you will only undo the work she's done this past week to try to get you out of her head."

I stopped the door with my foot as Whitney tried to slam it. "Just…take care of her for me. Make sure she doesn't go to a party and end up with the wrong guy—I worry about her getting hurt."

A humorless laugh came from Whitney's lips. "She's been with the wrong guy for the past few months. No one could hurt her worse than you have."

I already hated myself, but the self-loathing deepened. I didn't deserve to know she was okay, even if it was what I thought about twenty-four-seven.

"And you can bet that we'll be hitting lots of parties, where we'll meet tons of guys. Pretty soon you'll be nothing but a bad memory."

My phone rang, and when I went to look at it, Whitney took advantage and slammed the door, the lock clicking into place.

Mr. Hawthorne, of course. Most likely calling to tell me he'd worked out a settlement with Karen Walker. After discussing it with Aunt Tessa and Megan—since I thought she deserved to know before it was gossip—we'd decided to put out a press release about how excited we were to discover we had a new member of the family, and that we'd appreciate privacy as we got to know this miracle soul who gave us one more piece of Dad here on earth. It was over-the-top sugary bullshit, and no one would be giving us privacy, but at least we weren't busting our asses to hide it so it could blow up in our faces later.

Part of me even thought Dad might be proud. I wasn't sure where Mom would stand. Perhaps they'd both decided to be with people they loved, since they'd clearly fallen out of love with each other. Guess we'd never know.

I answered the phone, listening as Mr. Hawthorne finalized the details for the press release. He then let me know that Karen had signed the settlement. This weekend Megan and I were scheduled to meet our half sister, Avery. Since Megan was still mad at me over everything that'd happened with Lyla, she'd probably spend most of the time shaking her head and telling me, yet again, what a jerk idiot I was.

I was pulling out of my parking spot when I saw Lyla crossing to her place, her bulging backpack slung on both shoulders, her bright red hair in a bun, at least three pencils through it. I lowered the phone, no longer able to concentrate on anything Mr. Hawthorne said. She was as pretty as ever, but she didn't look good—stress hung on her features, and the way she dragged each step made me think she was sleeping about as well as I was.

She headed up the concrete staircase to her apartment, and I watched, longing and regret slowly suffocating me. I reached for my door handle, ready to jump out, apologize for being a giant fuckup, and beg her to take me back.

But then I remembered what Whitney had said. The last thing I wanted was to make things any harder for Lyla. So instead of soaking in her profile every second I could while wishing with everything in me for her to look my way, I shoved the gearshift into place and drove out of the parking lot.

The frayed string between us stretched further and further, until it snapped, severing everything we'd had for good.

Chapter Thirty-One

Lyla

"I don't know whether to be impressed or ashamed of us," I said to Whitney as I scraped together a bite of double-nut fudge ice cream from the container. Einstein stuck his head between us, trying to steal a taste, so I put him on the other side of me on the couch.

Whitney dragged her spoon across the remains, and then we'd officially polished off the entire carton. "I think it's impressive. We didn't even get brain freeze."

"But we've become a cliché," I said with a sigh. After Beck and I had our big blowup, I'd called Whitney in tears, no idea what else to do. She'd told me to hang tight and she'd come get me. Tessa dropped me off at a Starbucks—and she was at least nice enough to ask if I was absolutely sure I'd be okay there—and within a few hours, my roommate showed up to take me back to Boston.

On the way home she listened to me cry, rant, and lament the fact that I'd let my grades slip to spend time with a guy who didn't even want me. I'd wrapped my entire world up in a guy, like one of those girls I swore I'd never be, and in return he'd broken my heart into tiny, sharp pieces that jabbed me every time I tried to breathe.

Then she'd told me she and Matt were over, too. He'd finally responded to one of her many texts to say he had a girlfriend now, so he couldn't see her anymore, and to please stop calling and texting. Over the past few weeks, we'd perfected wallowing in pity and cursing the male species.

I rubbed my tummy. "And now I'm going to feel self-conscious when I have to slide down my skirt for the tattoo."

"Who cares? We gave up guys, remember?"

I tossed my spoon on the coffee table, satisfied with the loud *clank*. "Right."

Whitney paused, scrunching up her face the way she did when she couldn't recall something. "Or were we just going to go for nerdy guys? I forget what we decided last night. All those margaritas…"

"Now that you mention it, I think it was nerds."

Whitney licked off the back of her spoon. "Sexual chemistry is totally overrated. The hotter the guy is, and the hotter the sex is, the more likely they are to mesmerize you with their penis and then crush your heart."

I laughed, even though I sorta wanted to cry at the same time. "If you want, I know a guy who's super awful at kissing—the chin licker, remember? There's probably no sexual chemistry there. I bet it'd be horrible."

"Well, what are you waiting for?" Whitney nudged me with her elbow. "Give me his number."

We both erupted in laughter. But then it faded and it got quiet, and I knew she was thinking about Matt, and I was thinking of Beck, despite the fact that somewhere around margarita six or seven last night, we'd decided this was the week we were getting our shit together and forgetting about our "almost lovers." Obviously they were our lovers from a purely sexual standpoint, but we meant it on the deeper, apparently unrealistic level.

I glanced at the time. "You ready to hold my hand?"

"I'm there for you, babe," Whitney said without missing a beat.

I slung my arm over her shoulder in a side hug. We were sad saps, but we'd grown a lot closer through our mutual heartbreaks, and we'd already agreed to room together again next fall. And when I'd decided I still wanted to complete my bucket list and get my tattoo, she promised to hold my hand and distract me through the pain.

After all, the list was about me, not Beck, even if I'd thought he'd be with me to see it through to the end.

Despite a few missteps, the list had taught me a lot about myself. I liked my body better than I ever had, although I didn't like when that was the *only* part of me guys paid attention to. It didn't mean I couldn't show off my figure, or that I had to hide under bulky clothes. I liked color, loved my flowing skirts with their bright patterns, and my scarves made excellent headbands. It was okay to be different, and it was okay if not everyone got me. I could step out of my comfort zone and be bold. And I sure as hell wasn't boring.

The tiny flower I was getting inked on my hip would serve as a reminder of everything I'd learned my first year at college. So even though there were moments I wondered how I was going to survive the day when my heart ached so badly—and regardless of the hours I'd spent wondering if Beck and I would still be friends if we hadn't thrown sex into the mix—I didn't regret it.

I'd tried. I'd loved. I'd survived.

I was strong.

I was me.

Chapter Thirty-Two

BECK

Here I was playing in the regional final, just like I'd dreamed of doing since the start of the season, and I couldn't summon up an ounce of happiness. We'd won yesterday's game in overtime, thanks to a goal I'd made — a moment that should've been one of the best of my life — and it'd felt empty.

Since everything fell apart with Lyla, I felt empty all the damn time.

Instinct and years of training had gotten me to this point, but at this level, autopilot wasn't cutting it anymore. Last period I'd made sloppy mistakes, and UMass had caught up with less than a minute left in the game.

The ref blew the whistle — time out, our side. *Good. I need a minute. Although I'll probably just get chewed out.*

As I skated toward the bench, I tried to shake away the thoughts dragging me down. *Come on, head in the game.*

Don't think about her or you'll finish falling apart.

In spite of the weak pep talk, my gaze went to the stands. I'd stupidly scanned them before the game, hoping Lyla would miraculously show up. That she'd somehow know I needed her to be here and come to the DCU Arena to make playing seem worth it.

Of course she wasn't there, though—why would she be?

I thought about the evening we'd played hockey over spring break. How she'd known the perfect distraction to make me forget about everything else. How she'd joked that she had a future in the NHL, and I told her it would be cheering for me in the stands.

Pain lanced my heart. Instead of stepping away from the edge, I dove over. Thought about how she'd held my hand and encouraged me to not give up on my dreams. Ever since I'd found out Dad wasn't who I'd thought he was, I wondered why I'd give up what I wanted so he could have what he wanted. I was working to push past the bitterness and make peace with it, but the more I thought about it, the more I considered Lyla's assertion that my dad would choose my happiness over resenting a company he'd poured his heart and soul into. I also thought maybe she was right about keeping my options open.

Hell, what was I saying? She *was* right. Right about everything. I'd used my parents' disastrous relationship as an excuse and withdrawn when I should've fought for us. I'd been so sure I couldn't love her the way she deserved. But weeks away hadn't changed the way I felt about her. If anything, it only made me realize how much I loved her, and just how powerful love could be. I didn't know exactly what had happened with my parents' relationship or when it'd broken, but it didn't matter. Their mistakes—being scared—they were lame reasons not to take a chance with Lyla.

Lyla, who'd held me together when I was on the verge of falling apart. She knew the good and the bad, and she somehow loved me anyway.

She made me believe love was worth fighting for, and I just…I needed her. More than I'd ever needed anything, including hockey.

The revelation nearly sent me to my knees, especially since I'd ruined things so badly I wasn't sure I even had a chance at redeeming myself.

"Davenport?" Coach barked, and my teammates parted to leave me front and center.

Shit. I have no idea what he's been saying. "Yeah, Coach?"

"This is the last shot, and I need your head in the game. Do you even want this?"

I sucked in a deep breath, the cold air battling the heat blasting through me. *Time to get your shit together, Davenport. No more cop-outs, no halfway. All in.*

"Yes, sir! I'll put it in, Coach."

He batted me on the side of the head, told my teammates to get me the puck and block, and then it was time to make things happen. First I'd lead my team to victory, and then I'd fix everything else, no matter what it took.

My world zeroed in to my blades against the ice, the hockey stick in my hands, and the puck. My breaths sounded loud in my helmet. Adrenaline pumped through my veins and every muscle tensed, ready to spring into action.

The whistle blew, the puck hit the ice.

The defenders read the play and one of the UMass guys intercepted. I raced toward the swarm of bodies, focused on stopping them from scoring at all costs. Jeff stole the puck away and passed it to me. Cradling it with the end of my stick, I spun and made a fast break for our goal.

One point away from the Frozen Four.

One point till I could start putting the broken pieces of my life back together.

The seconds had to be in the single digit range now, so I pushed harder. Out of the corner of my eye, I caught the red and blue jersey of number 25. I threw out my elbow and he slapped at me, our sticks slamming together. But I still had the puck.

Using every ounce of strength I had left, I pushed forward, gaining speed, the goalie now the only thing between me and the net. I faked right, then aimed for the left corner and swung…

The goalie dove for it, spreading his legs and arms wide.

The puck slid through, crossing the line a mere second before the buzzer went off, signaling the end of the game. Sirens erupted, along with cheers from the crowd. The team rushed me, swarming the ice, and for a moment, I could hardly believe it. We'd done it. We were in the Frozen Four, with a chance at becoming national champions.

Cheers and the high of winning filled the locker room air, and the rest of the guys continued to celebrate as I rushed to shower and dress. When I burst out of the locker room, a large crowd waited. My phone bumped my thigh with every step, a steady reminder that my night was only beginning. The images on there had tortured me for days, but now I planned on using them to help make my case—I was going to need all the help I could get, and I was afraid it still wouldn't be enough.

If she won't give me another shot... I immediately shut down that thought, because I couldn't deal with even the possibility, not now that I knew how empty my life was without her. *I'll do whatever it takes to fix it, no matter how long it takes.*

"Beckett!" Megan barreled into me and I hugged her tight. Aunt Tessa nodded from behind her, looking completely out of place, but she'd come anyway. Ever since finding out the truth about Dad, she seemed to be trying extra hard with Megan and me. She'd even apologized for the things she'd said about Lyla and Mom, which I could tell had been hard for her to do.

"That was seriously awesome," Megan said. "I'll admit I covered my eyes there at the end, because I was so scared it wouldn't go in, but I saw the replay, and wow. I'm really happy for you. Still a tiny bit annoyed about *other* things, but happy."

Of course she had to get in that last jab. "Thanks," I said, and then I ruffled her hair since I knew she thought she was too old for it. On cue, she batted my hand away.

A man in his mid-thirties approached us. Through the years, I'd gotten pretty good at telling who the scouts were, and this guy fit the profile. The skill checklists in his hand confirmed it. The fact that he had on a Bruins cap sent my nerves into overdrive, and after the beating they'd taken during the game, short-circuiting was sure to follow. I needed to get it under control, because I didn't have time for that.

"Great game," he said, then stuck out his hand. "I'm Jeremy Alexander. Been watching you play for a while."

The line between my brain and mouth must've shorted out, too. I shook his hand, incapable of speech.

"That last period was a bit better than the first two."

Finally I found my voice. "Yes, sir."

"The pressure can mess with your head, but you pulled out of it when it mattered."

I wondered what he'd do if I said it wasn't the pressure, it was because of a girl. And that she was the same reason I'd turned it around there at the end, too. Even when she wasn't with me, she was. God, I'd been so stupid and blind.

The rest of the team spilled out, and their family and friends pushed in to see them, interrupting the conversation.

Under other circumstances, I would've tried to chat for a while and celebrate more with my boys, but my skin felt too tight and my feet grew desperate to bolt. The girl I loved was out there, and I needed to find her—I didn't want to waste one more day not having Lyla in my life. Funny how the thought of being denied a committed relationship now scared me a hundred times more than the alternative.

"Nice meeting you," I said to the scout, backing away before I got gridlocked and stuck here any longer. I turned to Megan and Aunt Tessa. "Thanks for coming to the game. But I gotta go."

I only hoped I wasn't too late.

Chapter Thirty-Three

LYLA

Okay, Whitney and I had a game plan for this. With my rapid heartbeat pounding through my head, I just couldn't remember what the hell it was. The people crowded around me weren't helping either. Add to that the memories from my first party here with Beck and this was a disaster waiting to happen.

I'd known there was a chance Beck would be at this party, just like Whitney knew Matt might be here with his new girlfriend, who I disliked on principle—I felt bad about it, but still. Honestly, the possibility of having to face him again was one of the reasons I'd worn my embroidered dress with my over-the-knee brown boots. *Oh yeah,* that *was part of the game plan. Show him what he's missing.*

As the music and multiple conversations in the Quad buzzed around me like a tornado, I stared at the back of the maybe-Beck guy. I thought I'd somehow *just know* if it were him, as if my body was so attuned to his it'd scream at me. It was screaming all right, my pulse now skittering under my skin, but it was still more of a that-*might*-be-him scream. With the dimmed lights, I could only make out that the guy was tall, the same build as Beck, and that his hat was black and possibly a Bruin's cap. What with us being in Boston, that wasn't even a sure sign it was him.

"Hey." Whitney extended me a red cup. "See any hotties?"

Maybe the one I'm desperately trying to get out of my head. I glanced at where maybe-Beck had been standing, but he'd gotten swallowed up in the crowd. The place was extra crazy tonight, so many people crammed inside it was hard to move, and if I hadn't stayed rooted in place, I doubted Whitney would've found me again. "Not really," I shouted over the music.

"Well, don't give up. We're at least finding a *possibility* tonight—that was what we agreed to. Our first step to get over those douchebags we're not mentioning."

Part of me wanted to ask, *What's the point?* There was only a month and a half of school left, and while I missed sex—I couldn't believe how much, considering it was such a little part of my life pre-Beck and his damn mind-blowing sex—I was done with casual hookups. For a while anyway.

Whit and I made our way through the mass of people, and when we caught a good vibe, or a cute enough guy smiled at us, we'd introduce ourselves. I forced myself to use the small-talk skills I'd learned over the past few months, and I was getting pretty good at managing it without embarrassment, if I did say so myself.

We'd just grabbed another round of drinks when Whitney

started up a conversation with a tall guy with bronze skin and black curly hair—most definitely more jock than nerd, despite last week's vow. Which left me to come up with something to say to his cute friend, Noah. He was also super tall, but more on the scrawny side, with a great, easy smile that instantly made me glad we'd stopped to chat.

My attention drifted when I caught sight of the black cap again. The guy glanced to the left, and my heart seized. Bruins cap. Beck's profile.

Beck.

He turned to talk to someone, and I let out a relieved breath when the someone was a guy instead of a girl. I thought it was one of his teammates, but the features were too hard to make out at this distance.

"…major?" Noah asked.

I glanced at him, taking a stab at the part of the question I'd missed. "Chemistry. I want to get a job in pharmaceuticals someday." *Like maybe at my sorta-ex-boyfriend's company, because that won't be awkward at all.* "You?"

"Math. I'm thinking engineer, but I haven't decided for sure yet."

Score! He totally fits the nerd requirement. He picked at something on his shirt. "Ugh, my dog sheds like crazy."

"My cat does, too. Pretty much anything dark-colored is like catnip to him."

Noah laughed. "Right? How do they know?"

Inwardly I did a happy dance that I'd figured out how to talk to guys so easily, but then I realized it was because I didn't care. Noah was a nice guy, and on paper, we'd probably be the perfect match. But my skin didn't hum around him, and maybe that'd change with time, but I could hardly focus on him when I knew Beck was somewhere in the room.

I glanced at the spot I'd seen him last, and there he was. Staring right at me.

Our eyes locked and a sharp pain shot through my chest. *I'm strong, I'm strong, I'm strong.*

We stared far past the polite range, and the blur of the crowd, music, and flashing lights faded into the background. Then Beck took a step toward me. Sure I was about to faint, I gripped Noah's arm like a lifeline, even though I'd been ignoring whatever he'd been telling me.

The muscles along Beck's jaw tightened, tension filling the planes of his perfect face. I worried I was reading too much into his expression, but I swore he paled, and he looked…well, absolutely miserable. Pretty much the way I'd felt since our big blowout, no matter how hard I tried to pretend otherwise.

Afraid I'd burst into tears, or worse—fling myself at him and beg him to take me back—I forced myself to turn away. "Sorry, I…" My brain was too hazy to come up with anything to say. For a brief moment I entertained the idea of kissing Noah to show Beck I was over him—to hurt him the way he'd hurt me—but I didn't want to be that girl.

I was me. I was strong. I was…aching, aching, aching.

I looked for Beck again, deciding I needed to at least see how he was doing and, if he'd actually talk to me, ask him if things were better with his family. Despite everything, I wanted him to be able to push past all his demons and be happy. It'd kill me to be near him and not reach for him, but somewhere buried underneath the rubble of our relationship was the friendship we'd started with, even though I knew it'd forever be mangled as well.

But he was gone, and suddenly I worried I'd never see him again, and then I wanted to sit down on the sticky, cup-littered ground and cry.

My phone vibrated against my hip. With the music, I hadn't even heard the chime. I pulled it out and read the text.

Beck: *Is that your bf?*

I stared at the words. Seeing his name on my screen again stirred up a tornado of emotions, and a giant lump rose in my throat.

What to say, what to say? Words tumbled through my mind, so many responses to such a simple question, most of which had nothing to do with the actual question. Slowly, I forced my thumbs into motion.

Me: *No. Just met him.*

Beck: *Conquest for the list, then?*

I glanced around, trying to see where he was. Noah smiled at me, and I felt rude for texting instead of talking. I lowered my phone. Let Beck stew.

But it was easier said than done—my hands twitched, my fingers burning with the desire to send a response, and finally, I couldn't stand it. Especially after that last text. What the hell kind of question was that anyway?

"Sorry, Noah, but could you excuse me for a second?" I took a few steps away from him, my emotions morphing from agony to anger, although my heart still ached like someone had put it through the wringer and then shoved it back in my chest.

He breaks my heart and then dares to ask me about conquests? Does he expect me to ask him the same? Give him a high five if we both leave with someone?

I must've only imagined the tormented expression on his face—stupid wishful thinking, or projecting, or whatever had caused my mind to play tricks on me. I typed my reply, which wasn't easy considering how badly my hands had started shaking.

Me: *It's none of your business. What are you trying to do to me?*

My phone chirped and I stared at the picture he'd sent me. Chemistry Cat with his glasses and bowtie. On the top it said: DO YOU HAVE 11 PROTONS? Then, underneath: BECAUSE YOU ARE SODIUM FINE.

A tight band formed around my chest, constricting further with each breath I attempted to take. I ran a hand through my hair, trying to figure out why he'd send that image to me. Was this his way of trying to be friends again? Like we could just go back to the way things were?

Obviously even a mangled friendship was too much to hope for—I'd never feel neutral enough toward him to pull it off. Not without lots and lots of time, and even with that, I wasn't sure.

My phone vibrated again. A picture of an adorable kitten with a silver gift bow on his head showed up on my screen. He was crouched down, eyes wide, with the caption: OMG! GETITOFFGETITOFFGETITOFF

Right after came a picture of a black cat behind a gray

and white one, his tongue out. ARE YOU LICKING ME? was across the top. Then, down by the black cat, SHH…JUST LET IT HAPPEN

> Beck: *This is what I do with my spare time now. I find these pictures that you'd love and end up staring at them while thinking of how stupid I am for letting you go. I'm so miserable I can hardly eat or sleep, and I despise that I even have to be around myself*

Tears sprung to my eyes. I clenched my jaw and blinked, trying to hold them back. I wanted to give in and tell him I'd been miserable, too, but I was afraid of what would happen after. Of being hurt again. There was overcoming your fears, and then there was not learning from your mistakes.

> Me: *You hurt me, Beck. Worse than anyone ever has. It's going to take more than a couple of chemistry jokes and cat pictures to make it okay.*

> Beck: *I know. That's why I'm willing to do whatever it takes. Including this…*

I looked around, trying to see what he was talking about. I didn't see him anywhere. The music died, and instead of another song starting up, dead silence followed. Even the conversations going on quieted at the stark contrast to the constant noise.

Then Beck jumped up next to the DJ booth, a micro-phone in his hand. "Lyla, I screwed up. I know I suck, and I don't deserve another chance, but I'm so damn sick of pre-tending I'm okay without you." He took a deep breath and then cleared his throat. "Because, baby..."

He glanced at the DJ, and a second later the familiar *bloop, bloop* noise sounded out. Beck stared across the crowd at me and raised the microphone to his lips. "You spin my head right round, right round—"

"What the hell is he doing?" Whitney asked, stepping up next to me.

I put my hands over my heart. It launched into motion, the erratic pumping stirring up a new wave of emotions, happy ones that battled to take over the sad. "He's singing our song."

Whitney winced when the rapping began. "He's really bad."

I laughed, although it came out half-sob. "I know."

There were cheers, and some boos, and a lot of people looking at each other like they didn't know how to react. When Beck pointed the microphone at the crowd for help, though, a large part of them sang along with him. Unlike karaoke night, the lyrics were blasting out of the speakers, too, helping when he didn't know the words and chose not to do the Kesha part.

As the song wound down, Beck crooked his finger at me and mouthed, "Please." The crowd seemed to turn as one to see who he was pointing at, and then there I was, suddenly the center of attention. My face heated, and speaking of "right round," my head was spinning. Judging from the wetness sliding down my cheeks I was also crying.

Of all the romantic gestures, I couldn't believe I was about to be won over by a badly done hip-hop song. Logical or not, though, the signs of swooning were all there. Likeliness of fainting? Shortness of breath? Hysterical rapture?

Check, check, and check.

Not to mention the way my heart beat faster and harder—if it could speak, it'd be saying Beck's name. It belonged to him and had for a long time, no doubt about it.

Love really was one of those things that made no sense when you tried to analyze it. I pushed my way through the crowd. A few of Beck's teammates helped clear a path, people moving out of their way much faster than they had done for me. They nodded as I walked past and a couple of them clapped me on the shoulder. Beck tossed the microphone to the DJ and jumped down next to me, his face adorably flushed.

"Wow, that was embarrassing," he said. "Pretty sure I'm not going to ever live it down with the guys, either, but if it worked…" He cupped my cheek. "I'm so sorry for everything—I was a pucking idiot!"

I bit back a smile at his choice of swearing. It was so perfect. Like his off-key singing onstage, the cat memes he'd sent, his face, and just everything about him.

"I love you, Lyla. More than I ever knew was possible. I've been so miserable without you. We won regionals tonight, but all I could think of was getting back to you so I could make things right. I panicked when you weren't at your apartment, and then your neighbor told me she thought you'd come here. When I saw you with that guy, I was terrified I was too late.

"Even as I told myself to leave you alone if you'd moved on and were happy, I knew I'd never be able to do it, because the fact of the matter is, you belong with me." His gaze locked onto mine, so much passion blazing in his eyes my heart forgot how to beat for a moment. "Please say something."

"You won regionals? So you're going to the Frozen Four?"

A surprised laugh fell from his lips and then he nodded. "Yeah. As long as you're in the crowd cheering for me as my girlfriend, none of this silly pretending anything less than that is enough." He brushed his thumb across the top of my cheek and intoxicating warmth spread from his touch and traveled through my core. "What do you say?"

For the first time since we'd parted, I felt like I could finally take a full breath again. "I'll be there. And I love you, too."

Relief flooded his features, and then he crushed me to him and kissed me like he meant to imprint himself on my very soul.

People cheered in the background, and I knew we were making a spectacle of ourselves, but I didn't care. I flung my arms around him and deepened the kiss, soaking in the feel of his body against mine, his strong hands gripping my waist, and how against all odds, I'd somehow ended up with the one thing I wanted most.

Chapter Thirty-Four

BECK

I finished putting the last box into Lyla's car and then turned to face her—she had on these sexy tiny denim shorts, a lacy white top, and a bright floral scarf wrapped around her ponytail, the ends hanging over her shoulder. She was so pretty that I couldn't help moving in for a kiss.

"Are you sure you won't take the Land Rover?" I asked. "I can get another car sent for m—"

"It's very nice of you to offer, but I'll be fine." She wrapped her arms around my waist, hugging me tightly, and I slid my hands in her back pockets.

"I just worry about you driving that far all by yourself, especially in this rust bucket you call a car. And suddenly a month seems like forever."

She tipped up her head and pressed her lips to my jaw. "I know. But I've got to at least visit my parents. Hopefully the new look and new me doesn't freak them out too much. Then I'll be in Canterbury, and before long, you'll probably be sick of me."

"Impossible."

Lyla glanced at her apartment complex. "I can't believe my first year of college is over. It was both easier and harder than I imagined it'd be." Her gaze moved to me. "And better in a lot of ways, too. And now it's over, I can't help feeling a little sad. But at least I don't have to wait till next fall to see you—I'd never survive."

"Right back at you." I wasn't sure what the future held, but I knew I was going to do whatever it took to keep Lyla. She was going to visit her parents for a month, and then she'd come live in Canterbury for six weeks while we both did internships for D&T Pharmaceuticals. She'd get job experience in the career field she hoped to be in one day, and I'd learn the ropes of the company.

We'd talked a lot about it, and she convinced me it was okay to take these next few years to figure things out—even with the company turning over to me, I could leave most of the decisions up to the board of trustees and have them fill me in on important transactions. I'd have to travel back and forth a bit, but she told me she'd come with me as much as possible. That way I could figure out if a position at D&T was the future I wanted, or if I should keep my focus on working toward the NHL.

Being in New Hampshire over the summer would also help me finish dealing with Mom and Dad's estate, as well as spend some time with Megan and Avery, who was a dang cute kid. At first I'd suspected Karen was only after money, but the more I got to know her, the more I saw why Dad must've liked her. Or maybe even loved her. Didn't mean I agreed with the way he'd gone about things, or that I was cool with him and Mom cheating on each other. Luckily, Megan was dealing better than I'd expected, despite the constant gossip, and I think a big part of that was how motherly Karen acted toward her. Aunt Tessa simply wasn't cut out for it, even though she tried, and I could never repay her for all her help. So at least I wasn't completely dreading going home.

Still, I knew life would be much easier to deal with if Lyla was there with us. "Megan's so excited about moving back to our home for the summer—she never stops talking about it. Are you sure you're ready to deal with her full time, too?"

Lyla grinned, the dimple in her cheek flashing. "We've already talked about how we can gang up on you when one of us needs to win an argument. Girl power and all that, you know."

I shook my head but laughed. "I knew introducing you two was a bad idea."

Six weeks of living with my amazing girlfriend. Then back to Boston in the fall, so we could work on finishing our degrees and I could help my team defend our championship title. With Lyla in the stands during the Frozen Four tournament, I'd played the best hockey of my life, and we'd won the championship game by three points. Taking her home with me afterward to properly celebrate had made the victory that much sweeter.

I rested my forehead against hers and sighed. "I love you so much."

"I love you, too." She covered my lips with her fingertips.

"But don't say good-bye or I might cry. I keep telling myself that it's only four weeks. Only four weeks."

"Only four weeks," I repeated. I pressed her tighter against me, desire instantly heating my veins. "I think I better drag you into the apartment and have my way with you one more time. Make sure number seven's been accomplished as many times as possible before your first year of college is officially over."

She bit her lip, and I knew I was about to get my way. I leaned down and kissed her neck to seal the deal. Her fingernails dug into my arms—man, I loved when she did that.

"But I… I still need to get Einstein," she said. "And Whitney's in the apartment, and…"

I slid my thumb under the waistband of her shorts, brushing the spot where her sexy tattoo was. Her sharp intake of breath told me I was on the right path.

"Once more for the road sounds good," she whispered, her voice rough. "You know, I've never done it in a car before."

"We can't have that, can we?"

"But we'd need to go somewhere more secluded."

I scooped her up and placed her in the passenger side of the Land Rover. I knew just the place. And since it was going to be four long weeks before we got to be together again, I planned on making every last second count.

Acknowledgments

Another book down, and another awesome group of people to thank for all of their help. Thanks to Amanda Price for listening to my idea, giving me the courage to put it down on paper, encouraging me whenever I needed it and getting me through a lot of freak outs, and for reading the first draft when I was terrified to show it to anyone. Thanks to Melissa West, Megan Erickson, and Lia Riley for also reading it before it was as shiny, and for telling me that you laughed a lot while reading. Extra thanks to Melissa for reading scenes over again to help me play this or that, and for your friendship over the years. Big thanks to the amazing Anne Eliot for always being there, whether it's mood boosting or talking character arcs (I'm still never outlining beforehand, NEVER! Hehe) and for being my travel buddy and celebration meals together.

Thanks to Entangled Publishing and Alycia Tornetta and Stacy Abrams for being excited to genre-skip with me when

I want to try something new. Special thanks to Alycia for pushing me to make this book better, learning more about hockey with me, and making me think (even when I really didn't want to). Thanks to the cover designers, publicists—you're amazing Debbie Suzuki!—marketing team, and the other Entangled authors. I'm so happy and grateful to be part of such a supportive network.

Huge thanks to Janette Derucki for chatting with me about all things hockey and answering a lot of rambling texts. Thanks to Sophia Henry for the always-inspiring Hot Hockey God Friday. And to the rest of the girls in the TZWNDU book club, you make me laugh, celebrate my writing milestones with me, and are the absolutely coolest book club EVER!

I'd also like to thank the CKM for their support, as well as my sister, April, who listens to my writing dilemmas despite how busy she is. Thanks to Wordsmith Publicity, along with all the bloggers and readers who've helped spread the word about my books. And extra big thanks to my readers in general. You all rock!

And last, but definitely not least, thanks to my family, who suffers through burned meals, takeout meals (which they highly prefer to burned), and general chaos, so that I can get my writing and editing done. Especially to my husband, who always picks up the slack and has been one of my top supporters from the beginning. Love you!

About the Author

Cindi Madsen is a USA Today bestselling author of contemporary romance and young adult novels. She sits at her computer every chance she gets, plotting, revising, and falling in love with her characters. Sometimes it makes her a crazy person. Without it, she'd be even crazier. She has way too many shoes, but can always find a reason to buy a pretty new pair, especially if they're sparkly, colorful, or super tall. She loves music and dancing and wishes summer lasted all year long. She lives in Colorado (where summer is most definitely NOT all year long) with her husband and three children.

You can visit Cindi at: www.cindimadsen.com, where you can sign up for her newsletter to get all the up-to-date information on her books.

Follow her on Twitter @cindimadsen.